Praise for *The Art of Leaving*

"Stothard gets her talons into you . . . read it for its beguiling heroine and sparky prose." SEBASTIAN SHAKESPEARE, *Tatler*

"Anna Stothard's third book, after the much-praised *Isabel and Rocco* and *The Pink Hotel*, confirms her talent: the prose here can be transfixingly good," *The Independent*

"A stunningly accurate and chilling account of the acquiring of emotional wisdom, with vividly drawn characters," KATE SAUNDERS, *The Times*

"A witty, beguiling and increasingly poignant novel about the scars – physical and psychological – that make us who we are." STEPHANIE CROSS, *The Lady*

"I would recommend it to anyone who likes being told a very good story," *NewBooks*

"Anna Stothard's third novel cements her place as one of Britain's best young authors . . . Stothard's lush, dreamy prose is given full rein . . ." KAITE WELSH, *The Literary Review*

Praise for *The Pink Hotel*

"Astonishingly good . . . Stothard's writing is accomplished and very engaging." KATE SAUNDERS, *The Times*

"Matters of personal identity underlie an exhilarating ride through LA's seamier side in the company of a hard-bitten yet highly engaging protagonist." ROSS GILFILLAN, *Daily Mail*

"An elegant noirish mystery." AMANDA CRAIG, *The Independent*

"A gently transgressive, transatlantic quest that conjures up both the languid heat of LA and the confusions of a young woman on the cusp." *The Lady*

"Anna Stothard's descriptions are almost like a painting – the reader finds themselves slap bang in the middle of the America that is rarely shown in film or novels." ANNE CATER, *NewBooks*

"Anna Stothard's dark debut *Isabel and Rocco*, written while the author was still at school, was a McEwan-esque tale about two teenage siblings left to fend for themselves. Her second novel, set amongst the naval-gazers of California, proves no less precocious." EMMA HAGESTADT, *The Independent*

"A beautiful book." ANNA PAQUIN, RED *magazine*

Praise for *Isabel and Rocco*

"Anna Stothard's pre-university debut is dazzling . . . surly and oversexed, vulnerable and murderous . . . it is remarkably accomplished" GERALDINE BEDELL, *The Observer Review*

"Stothard's claustrophobic and compelling atmosphere of sadistic sexual fizz between her two main characters keeps the reader gripped" *The Times*

"Sinister debut from an author who shows serious promise. The plot has echoes of Ian McEwan's *The Cement Garden* – two children mysteriously left alone by their parents." JO CRAVEN, *Vogue*

"Rainy streets, kindly but inept teachers, rotting food and the highly seductive, just-surfacing, notions of forbidden sex – Stothard describes them all brilliantly" CAROLYN HART, Juice Magazine

"A dark tale of *enfants terribles* set in North London, Isabel and Rocco revolves around a brother and sister with an unhealthily obsessive relationship" MARIANNE BRACE, Harpers & Queen

"With shades of *Lord of the Flies*, Stothard has produced a chilling and haunting work" ANNABEL VENNING, *Daily Mail*

ANNA STOTHARD

THE MUSEUM OF CATHY

SALT

CROMER

PUBLISHED BY SALT PUBLISHING 2016

2 4 6 8 10 9 7 5 3 1

First published in Great Britain in 2016 by
Salt Publishing Ltd
12 Norwich Road, Cromer, Norfolk NR27 0AX United Kingdom

www.saltpublishing.com

Salt Publishing Limited Reg. No. 5293401

A CIP catalogue record for this book is available from the British Library

ISBN 978 1 78463 082 9 (Paperback edition)
ISBN 978 1 78463 083 6 (Electronic edition)

Typeset in Neacademia by Salt Publishing

Printed and bound in Great Britain by Clays Ltd, St Ives plc

To Sally Emerson

A<small>N ELEPHANT SKULL</small> *and a swallow rested on a cabinet of moths, all specimens of natural history that didn't have a place in the museum downstairs. The bird was particularly beautiful, three inches tall, with an ochre neck tapering down into forked blue wings. It had glossy black eyes that Cathy could have sworn just blinked at her.*

A few corridors over, a gallery the size of a tennis court contained thousands more stuffed birds so if this one was magically twitching back to life perhaps the matronly pelicans were also preening, the flamingos stretching their legs, the penguins sneezing and the two hundred hummingbirds rustling their feathers ready to seek revenge for the decades in which they'd been prodded and observed. Cathy smiled at the thought and then caught her breath when the swallow chirped twice, its feathered throat vibrating: it was not a specimen, after all. It looped down from the shelf and sailed past a cabinet of dragonflies to land on a pile of science journals.

Cathy was not easily spooked. She would walk first into fairground haunted houses and swear on people's lives without blinking, yet as the swallow looked for an escape route her hands were shaking. Trapped birds, her mother would say, were a warning.

"He likes you," Tom said from the doorway. She didn't immediately turn towards him, instead reaching over a desk to open the window for the swallow. A low hum of jazz music and laughter lifted up from a party in the museum's public galleries two floors below.

"He's not in a position to be choosy." Her face was still tilted away from Tom as he stepped into the room. The bird remained poised and stared directly at Cathy from its shelf. Tom adjusted his glasses and did the same. She looked new but familiar in her green silk evening dress, as if she'd discarded a layer of herself and climbed out raw. Her hands were shaking and when she eventually shifted her face in Tom's direction she revealed a bruise forming on her eye and a little blood on her mouth.

The swallow darted off across the room again, making them both flinch, still not heading for the window but soaring down from the table to a cabinet full of Monarch butterflies, where it shat a pool of white that dribbled down the glass.

The creature flapped its wings while treading air, its body curled into the shape of a comma. Cathy's skin had a feverish sheen to it. She licked a droplet of blood off her top lip with her tongue.

"Are you going to tell me what happened to you tonight?" said Tom. "I've missed you."

A Kissing Beetle

THE PAST IS not stable. The act of remembering changes us, and our whole lives can be re-written in a day. First thing the morning before the party she had paused in the doorway of the Berlin Natural History Museum and smiled good morning to a *Brachiosaurus* skeleton, his long neck skimming up to the atrium's glass ceiling. Cathy's dress for the evening's party was already dry-cleaned and hanging up at work but she carried high heels past fossils and polar bears across the marble floor.

It was going to be another humid day. Botanists, technicians and research fellows plodded through the museum while a cleaner dusted a glass case of dodo bones. Cathy turned left from the atrium into the darkness of a solar system exhibition with nine football-sized planets around a sun that was, misleadingly, exactly the same size as the planets. A day on Venus takes 243 earth days, a poster said. Jupiter takes 9.8 hours. Teenagers in particular congregated excitedly at the bottom of these stairs every day to kiss in the darkness. Cathy liked to imagine the teenagers aroused by the idea of their entire universe once being contained in a single, unimaginably hot point in space, but they probably just liked sneaking off into the dark.

Cathy wore a white shirt, tailored trousers and ballet slippers, her long auburn hair tucked neatly behind both ears. She twisted a coiled snake engagement ring on her left ring finger as she paced up a curved staircase towards the locked doors of various laboratories and collection rooms. Gallery and corridor windows were flung open in this uncanny summer heat, trying to dilute the smells of hot fur and preservation chemicals. She pushed into her office, a long room with a low ceiling cluttered with furniture and an ever-changing array of specimens that did not fit downstairs. Semi-broken office chairs were piled in the same corner as a stuffed owl while an elephant skull was perched on one of the many green cabinets arranged around the room, packed with everything from Atlas Moths the size of a baby's head to Pigmy Moths smaller than a comma in this sentence.

She sat down at her desk in front of the cedar wood tray of Deathshead Hawkmoths with orange underwings and skull shapes on their abdomens, bad omens throughout time. Cathy loved her rows of tidy pinned bodies with their fragile costumes, but she was equally besotted with the empty spaces in between each specimen. It was in these gaps that order existed. She believed the beauty of museums, like maps and human relationships, was in distance as much as connection.

She'd woken up next to Tom that morning and left him sleeping in their one bedroom flat with white floorboards in the south-eastern part of Berlin, Neukölln, an area full of battered launderettes and Turkish cafés where they'd lived for the last four years. She was English and Tom was American, part of the tapestry of exiles and drifters that made up the city. When Tom was asleep he looked like some evolutionarily superior species with his white teeth, square jaw and tanned face, his thin eyebrows giving him a perpetually amused expression. The moment he woke up he would start fiddling with his often-broken spectacles, shifting his weight from foot to foot and chain smoking, but asleep he was pristine. The flat had the empty atmosphere of a holiday cottage. The centrepiece was a wrought iron bed that was more of a disorderly pet because it made such a noise. Tom slept without moving but Cathy conducted nightly conversations with it. The frame groaned when she stretched, the mattress squeaked when she wriggled. Sex was a threesome, with the bed the most vocal participant. It seemed to mock them when they got off rhythm. They'd roll onto the floor but it still felt as if the bed were collaborating somehow.

As she sat down at her desk she saw a cardboard box about the size of her hand in the far corner, next to a microscope. The brown package must have come in early this morning or after she'd left work last night. She was glad that there was no one else in the room just then, or she was sure her colleagues would have been disturbed by the sound of her heartbeat.

Cathy slid the package nervously towards her body. She had published two journal articles on hawkmoths, so people did occasionally send specimens for her to identify or add to the museum's collection, but instinctively she knew the brown box wouldn't contain a moth. Her hands shook. Saliva filled her mouth. She slit the duct tape lengthways and twice horizontally with the end of a pair of scissors, opening the flaps to disclose polystyrene. She reached her right hand in to find a white box, nudging the lid off with her thumb: something padded in newspaper.

She unwrapped the layers to reveal a one-inch nugget of luminous amber that felt cool between her thumb and forefinger. She held it up to the light. Inside the amber sat a

Panstrongylus megistus, a Kissing Beetle, its slender head suffocated in resin. One antenna appeared to twitch as if reacting to Cathy's warm skin. Timeless creatures, shiny bullets of time, they were called Kissing Beetles because their habit was to bite sleeping humans in the soft tissue around the lips and the eyes. There was no label or letter of explanation, but she knew who this message was from.

❧

Daniel clenched and stretched his fingers, chlorinated water slicking down wrist hairs under the cuff of his hotel dressing gown. He had arthritis and enjoyed swimming more than fighting now, yet when he looked at his hands he thought fondly of hushed air and the sting of glove-burned flesh. A first punch that hit the ridge of his opponent's cheek, the sound of split bone but no time to be pleased about it. He ran fingers through his damp hair.

On the table was a fossilised sea eagle claw, an inch of chocolate brown bone neatly attached to a shard of finger. The claw had a little restoration at its tip but was otherwise immaculate. Cathy had told him once that a mouse's forelimb, a whale's flipper, a bat's wing and a human arm share almost the same pattern of bones. His own gnarly hands were as much ancestors of the raptor as a bat's wing.

Daniel's throbbing knuckles gave him a sense of unease. He was probably anticipating the breaking of the city's heat wave, maybe a storm after days of humidity. He was not used to this new freedom available to him, the knowledge that he could move around as he pleased. He touched the tip of the claw with his forefinger and thought of Cathy's lithe and bony hands with a seashell ring at the base of her middle finger. *For a decorative fuck you,* she'd once said.

⚜

Cathy unfolded the newspaper pages that the Kissing Beetle had been wrapped in and studied them. It was yesterday's copy of the German newspaper *Die Welt,* with half an article on how motorway tarmac was buckling near Abensberg in Lower Bavaria because of the heat. A school bus had hit a crash barrier, killing twelve children. In the torn left corner of the page, pasted on top of the newsprint, was a fragment of a sticker that said:

ments of
Shiro,
eakfast!

Cathy lifted this bit of information to get a closer look at the words. A complimentary newspaper with breakfast. There was a chain of hotels called Shiro; several were in Berlin. The hairs on her neck stood on end. There was no postmark on the cardboard box, but she ran her fingers across the deep grooves he'd made while writing her name on the top. It had been four years since Daniel had sent her an object like this. The palms of her hands were sweating.

Windows were open around the room, but none appeared to let in much of a breeze. Her office was right at the top of the museum, looking out on the front lawn. Peaking up above hotels and blocks of flats to her left, she could just see Berlin's TV tower glinting like a giant disco ball in the sky. Most of Berlin's old museums were trapped on their own island in the

7

city centre, but the Natural History Museum was a lone wolf up near the university and the central train station. It was a long building with a flat roof, the façade decorated with arched windows and pollution-grey sculptures that hid a puzzle of old and newly renovated wings behind. She could hear tourists and children outside the window, plus the chants of protesters who had been lingering on the front lawn recently, objecting to the museum's acceptance of sponsorship from an oil company. Inside the office there was just a focused hush of curators bent over trays of ladybugs or computer keyboards. She closed her eyes and moth wing-patterns, colourful circles and zigzags, danced on the back of her eyelids.

Cathy removed a little brass key from the pages of her *Encyclopaedia of Insects* on the shelf and slipped it into the cedar wood doors of a cabinet underneath her desk. This department of the museum had been modernised a few years ago and most of the antique storage units had either been sold off or warehoused to make way for the green steel that currently filled the office. Cathy had saved one old cabinet for herself, four feet wide and two feet tall with a splintered crack down its panelled double doors. She kept it underneath her desk, but it had never contained the articles on phylogeny, biogeography or wing polymorphism advertised on the labels.

The doors creaked open and Cathy paused to make sure her colleagues were all busy pinning wings or dissecting abdomens, making tiny cuts between heart pulses in their own thumbs. One of the many things she loved about working in natural history museums was that she would never be the only person with strange archiving habits. There was a man in the whale storeroom who had a drawer marked 'string too small for further use'.

8

Inside Cathy's cabinet were drawers full of more than two hundred small memory-objects she'd been collecting since she was a child. The archive began the winter before she turned ten, in coastal Essex where she was born, with a pristine mouse skull she found near the beach. It was a perfect specimen, almost entirely intact and bleach-white, with a delicate jaw that still opened. The collection spanned all the places she'd lived: Essex, until she escaped to Los Angeles age twenty-two, and now four years in Berlin with Tom. It ended a few days ago with a sketch of her mouth that Tom had made on a restaurant napkin. Her mouth was wide open, the slight gap between her front teeth exaggerated by the perspective. Between these two edges of her life were birthday candles, train tickets and childhood dolls. She did not like the turmoil of memories constantly poised in her mind, synapses and chemicals shifting their weight according to new moods and often threatening to collapse or disband. She could exert control over her memories here, and close the door on them.

She had a number of objects that, like the Kissing Beetle, were connected to Daniel. She had a molar tooth that he knocked from her mouth when she was twenty, which made her smell blood each time she looked at it. She had a clump of her hair in a matchbox that had been pulled from her head when she was twenty-one. She had a seaside-arcade stuffed white tiger with wonky eyes that didn't just allow her to remember being in love for the first time but performed some alchemy of time and place, so that she tasted Mr Whippy ice cream and stubble against his lips. Other objects were threats, which she'd been sent in the post after she left him. She had auk and gannet skulls, starfish and carved boats and seagull feathers. These objects made the hairs on the back of her neck stand on end and her skin heat up. The last gift she'd been sent before the Kissing Beetle was over four years ago, an angel shark jawbone with teeth sharp as nails, after which the gifts had stopped.

Her private museum's purpose was not to escape her past, but to control it. Cathy had grown up near a bird sanctuary in one of twelve holiday chalets that were relics of an ill-advised Essex holiday camp from the Fifties. A *floating caravan park*, her mother called their street. She spent her childhood exploring coastal marshland full of migrating terns, salt stiff grass and North Sea tides. She spent it trawling bracken, crunching salty white grass under her Wellington boots in search of twisted driftwood and gems of sea glass. The twelve chalets on her street all had shaky insulation and noisy plumbing, not built for winter living, yet at some point her father had decided he didn't want to belong to any form of society other than The Essex Bird Watching Society. So they'd lived in this isolated landscape all the year round, from before Cathy could remember. She'd grown up tracking the tides on a chart in her bedroom, mindful of her nervous mother's theory about how all the buildings on their street would one day just lollop over the shrubby wall of marsh and out to sea in the middle of the night. It was never silent in Lee-Over-Sands. Even the word sounded like a bad incarnation, the O forced your mouth open but then you had to hiss and finish off the name. In the wrong mood, when birds appeared to hang from the sky and mist fell too quickly over the shifting tides, it made you think of spirits. It was a place where nature ruled. Cathy would scream her bike down the gravel road over the seawall between the sea and the town and float the high tides in her orange rowing boat that washed up in front of her deck when she was eight.

At first her objects were curiosities from the natural world around her, rather than the anchors to specific emotions or memories that they became. Everyone collected things in Lee-Over-Sands. Window ledges all down the street were laden with driftwood, bones and glass jars of seashells. Even in the many near-derelict houses where nobody came for years and years at a time, mounds of sea glass and bird skulls still sat on ledges and decks, along with feathers and mouldy twists of rope. Scavenged things were just curiosities for Cathy then and memories were absorbed inside her. A dirty rabbit's foot on a gold key chain did not sum up her mother's essence. Her father was not epitomized by a small pair of binoculars with smudged lenses and two empty miniature bottles that had once contained Bombay Sapphire gin. Cathy was merely a hoarder before she turned ten; she was just a beachcomber then, a filler-upper of drawers and pockets.

A Snake Ring

TOM PUT A paper cup of black coffee and a fistful of sugar packets down on her desk and adjusted his glasses, which were held together with tape at one side. He kissed her warm neck and inhaled the smell of shampoo and sweat. She touched the engagement ring on her finger as he kissed her, as if checking it was still there.

"It's too hot again," Tom said, and tucked a strand of hair behind Cathy's ears. Cathy wasn't good with heat, she became sullen and veins rose to the surface of her skin. She was designed for rainy English summers.

"Morning," she smiled and kissed his left hand where it now rested on her shoulder. She began to pour sugar packets into her coffee. She did it almost haughtily, as if daring him to stop her or tell her it was unhealthy.

She arrived at work hours before he did, because he was incapable of being on time and she was incapable of being late. As he cycled towards the museum his creased shirt would flap out behind him and an unlit cigarette hung in the side of his mouth, ready to be smoked the moment he parked his bike. He usually took his feet off the pedals as he drove over a canal at *Hallesche-Tor Bridge*, talented at finding pleasure in small moments. He tried not to sound his bell at tourists near Checkpoint Charlie and continued on up over the river Spree. He smoked his first cigarette of the day on the museum's lawn and then bought coffee from the cafeteria to take to Cathy.

She was his favourite subject to sketch, parts and pieces in countless notebooks along with whatever whale ribs or spikes of a Stegosaurus's backbone he was studying at the time. They'd been together five years, four years in Berlin and one before that in Los Angeles, where they'd met, but still he didn't feel he'd ever entirely captured her likeness. Her perfectly symmetrical eyes and thin lips were not immediately pretty. It was a blank-canvas face, only visible when she was animated or engrossed. When something interested her, she abruptly became beautiful but she could never fake this kind of engagement. He always worked quickly: the curve of her ears, her high forehead with its inch-long scar from slipping in a pile of construction material when she was twelve. Her body was covered in lingering flaws from tumbling into gravel and playing red rover with older boys as a child. She'd been in a car crash when she was a teenager, one of many examples of a shitty childhood she didn't like to talk about much. The marks and misalignments had shocked him when he first saw them, but now fascinated him: lines on her shoulder from diving into a bramble bush, scars on her knuckles and elbows and forehead from the car accident, her past quite different from Tom's careful urban upbringing. She'd fractured her metatarsal bone jumping off a wall as a kid and had a tiny bump on the outside of her right foot that made her flinch if you touched it. When he sketched her feet he could never get that bump exactly right.

"The adult body contains over 100,000 miles of blood vessels," Tom said as she continued to insert pins around the moth on her desk, pursing her mouth while contemplating the truth of his statement. She spent her days spreading moth wings, running pins through their thoraxes and trapping them in perpetual low flight.

"Fact. The largest diamond in the world is ten billion trillion trillion carats," she offered. She took the next moth body from an envelope, ready to pin it.

"Sounds unlikely." They played this game in supermarket queues and over dinner, on public transport and in bed, fact or fiction, teasing each other and storing up details of life to share.

"It's true, scout's honour. It's a star named Lucy, after 'Lucy in the Sky with Diamonds', 50 light-years from the earth," she said.

"You were never a scout. You don't have any team spirit." He touched the vertebrae on her neck, peaking up like islands after a flood. "The tongue of a blue whale weighs the same as a fully grown female African elephant," he said. Because Cathy's hair was dark red you would have thought her eyes would be brown, but in fact they were blue and they illuminated in flashes. Tom joked that she made an excellent *seventh* impression; she was a subtle thing that snuck up on people.

There had been a group of acrobats practising nearby when he'd asked her to marry him last week in the *Hasenheide* Park opposite their flat and gave her his grandmother's ring, a snake with a ruby in its head. A passer-by offered to take a photo of them afterwards. The resulting image chopped both their heads off, but they got the photo developed anyway and it was currently propped up on their kitchen table. You can just see their decapitated bodies and a child acrobat doing a handstand in the background.

"True," she said. "A flock of starlings is called a murmuration."

"True. A crow can remember human faces and hold a grudge," he said.

"False. Legend," she said. She smiled up at him. "Nowhere in the Humpty Dumpty nursery rhyme does it actually say that the character is an egg."

"False. It must say he's an egg. It's true about the crows, though. Never piss off a crow."

"They don't teach nursery rhymes in California? Philistine."

"Lunch at 2.30 today?"

"Perfect," she said, taking another sip of sugary coffee. She turned her head to kiss his hand again. "And I would have made an excellent scout, thank you."

"You would have led a meticulous regiment."

Sometimes Cathy would go through his sketchbooks after he'd drawn something, and neatly label the anatomy of his messy drawings. The lack of structure in his books worried her. She liked order. That her own pelvis and the toes of an *Ankylosaurs* shared the same A4 page went against her instinct for cataloguing life. So she would sit at the little table they used as a desk in their flat and frown as she labelled her own *ear canal, pinna, cartilage.* Neat arrows. The same with a hummingbird's skeleton: *ulnar, radius, thoracic, caudal, lumbar vertebrae.* She said the names as she wrote them. She labelled the sketches he made of her long legs, tangled amongst cheap sheets on their bed. *Tibia,* she printed. *Cathy's fibula. Cathy's femur. Cathy's coccyx, Cathy's sacrum.*

When Tom left her office, Cathy slipped the Kissing Beetle safely into a top drawer next to the sketch of her half-open mouth. She kept her private museum at work because Tom couldn't see a drawer or a notebook without opening it;

he was insatiably curious, which she loved about him, but not in this particular instance. She had never shown him her objects because she had no desire for her past and future to mingle. The oppressive pleasure and stillness she found in the indexed memories was not something she wanted to share, even with someone she loved as much as Tom. Her respect for objects was almost spiritual, but not communal.

One of her favourite objects in the cabinet was a green cocktail umbrella, which she'd been spinning in her hand the first time she ever spoke to Tom. They'd been sitting on a wall looking out on Venice Beach in mid-December, just before Christmas, their bare feet in the Californian sand. She'd been in Los Angeles three months then and had not yet reinvented herself since leaving Daniel. She was soft around the edges, newly hatched and unsure. She'd thrown away all her damp-seeped clothes, her marshy tracksuits and oxidised hoop earrings that smelt of home, then bought new clothes from a charity shop on Hollywood and Western. She could go for weeks without speaking about anything much except what sort of Starbucks coffee she would like. For months didn't touch anyone or, it seemed, anything. Concrete and plywood and metal all had the same texture for her in Los Angeles, the same level of heat and wetness. Her concession to human contact was going to these cheap massage parlours that smelt of dumplings, where she'd lie naked on futons in rooms cordoned off by fraying curtains. She allowed Thai women to unbutton her pressure points, twisting their elbows into knots between her shoulder blades and opening up her joints with their small fingers. They did not mention her scars. She missed wading into mud with the tide licking her toes, as if her body was physically detoxing from the glut of sensation that had marked her life until then.

Her university in Essex had arranged for her to do a work placement at the Los Angeles Natural History Museum, cataloguing ice age insect fossils dug up from the La Brea tar pits. She had begged for one of the few jobs they offered abroad but once she arrived, she'd made no effort to make any friends. It shouldn't have been a great surprise that nobody spoke to her when she turned up at the museum Christmas party in Venice Beach three months into the job. Regretting the numerous buses it took her to get there, she bought a cocktail and sat outside on a low wall at the beach's edge, sipping her drink and twirling her cocktail umbrella. Eventually a blond man with wide perfect teeth and blue eyes came and sat down next to her, lighting a cigarette and offering her one.

She declined. He smelt of beer and started rambling tipsily about how he was spending Christmas with his family in Palm Springs, about all its complicated dynamics involving disapproval and love affairs and money. Cathy had smiled politely and wondered why he was talking to her. She expected that he'd just wanted to sit down for a smoke, and she happened to be there. When he asked about her Christmas plans she lied and told him she was going back home to Essex for Christmas; she didn't want to say she had nowhere to go. She and this first incarnation of Tom watched the Santa Monica Pier in the distance, a Ferris wheel's pink and blue light reflecting a puddle of sherbet colour onto the otherwise dark water. Soda cans were skimming the pavement as hot air sprayed down into Los Angeles from Nevada and Utah, spreading wildfires and anxiety, then exhaling into the sea. The atmosphere was static. People smoked cigarettes on fire escapes and the balconies of seaside apartment buildings, watching the stormy sea, and the sidewalk cafés were crowded.

Homicides and suicides spike during Santa Ana winds, Tom had said after a pause, in his Californian drawl. Her sundress kept spilling up in the hot blustering air and she kept tucking it under her thighs. She took off her baseball cap and then regretted it, because he might ask about the scar on her forehead. It went from the far edge of her right eyebrow straight up to her temple and she always covered it with make-up before she left the house, but it was still visible, one of the mementos from her old life that she couldn't put in a box and close the door on.

That's what these are, Santa Ana, he said of the wind, and appeared not to notice her face.

Cathy spun her little green cocktail umbrella and took a sip of her drink. It tasted of gin and cinnamon. Three elves and a man dressed as Mrs Claus spilled out of the bar behind them. Tom lit another cigarette from the last but did not appear nervous, merely overflowing with energy. He moved constantly, his foot tapping the floor, his thumb rolling over the lighter in his hand. She'd seen him around the museum: he was a successful palaeontologist who'd already published various papers. He had a square jaw and a thin mouth that was often smiling. His glasses usually had some tape around one of the arms to keep them together. A cheer went up in the crowd behind them, so Cathy and Tom turned to watch the scene. A drunken man with dreadlocks had fallen off his skateboard, but Cathy's gaze immediately landed on three older men drinking beer at a crowded sidewalk café nearby. One of the men had a side parting and thick eyebrows; another was deeply tanned, with a three-inch beard. This bearded man appeared to be staring in Cathy's direction. The third man in the trio had his back to her, but his perfectly still, uncommonly broad shoulders and curly black hair brought a lump to Cathy's throat. It couldn't have been Daniel, but she still felt sick.

He had found out where she was almost immediately, within weeks of her leaving Essex. She didn't know exactly how he managed it. He didn't come for her but he continued to give her gifts, as he had done when they were together. First a tropical shell had arrived at The Los Angeles Natural History Museum for her, three weeks after she arrived in her new city. From a white box full of tissue paper, she'd unwrapped a pretty Ramose Murex shell with three jagged Mohawks of solidified flesh sticking out from a coiled body. Turning it over, she saw that the shell's open underside was so shiny it appeared wet, the lips much pinker than her skin as she ran her fingers along the slit. She pretended to herself that it must have been delivered to the wrong person. A week later the skull of a seagull had turned up, neatly wrapped in chocolate brown paper with a blue label from an expensive shop called Deyrolle in Paris that they'd once visited together. The seagull's head was smooth, but its beak reminded her of a dagger.

There was never a note, but other objects followed, sent to the museum and then also – more worryingly – to her flat. A fish spine, a Trapezium Conch, a carved rowing boat. She was insane to have accepted a single one of these objects, yet she did. Daniel had no business fastening her to him with voltaic things, changing the external brain of her an hive. She should have thrown them away, but she placed each gift in her shoeboxes and suitcases. He knew her devotions, after all, and despite the fear each object brought with it she obediently added these gifts to the narrative of her life.

In the Santa Ana winds, sitting next to Tom, tears had pricked up in Cathy's eyes. She didn't think the older man with curly hair in the sidewalk café was actually Daniel, but tears came into her eyes because the thought occurred to her. These mixed feelings almost made her want to turn to the lazy-limbed and confident near stranger to her right and tell him how sounds used to echo on the marshes where she grew up, and how tides reinvented the landscape every morning. How, if you sang a song or shouted, birds would wheel up from the ground right into the sky and start scavenging. How she would stand naked on the marsh and scream, because there was no one around for miles. How it was never the same world twice and the tides marched like ghosts up and down the marshes. How pleased she was to have got away from the landscape of her past. She wanted to tell him how her childhood had been ruled by the moods of the sea and the sky.

But she didn't tell him anything, just tried to unclench her jaw and breath deeply. She was a new person now, she told herself. Although at that point her objects were still all jumbled together in shoeboxes with little order to them, Cathy was beginning to see that she could keep her past locked up and out of sight if she wished. She could put a lid on the guilty girl: lock her up in a drawer like a specimen. Instead of pouring out her secrets to Tom, Cathy just swallowed hot desert air from the Santa Ana winds, as they merged with the salty beach air of the ocean in front of her. She held her tiny green cocktail umbrella tight between her thumb and forefinger.

A flamboyance is a group of flamingos, she had said to Tom, instead of baring her soul to him. She then cringed at the randomness of the phrase. She wiped her nose with the back of her hand as she used to do as a kid. Tom replied:

That's not true.

It is.

A flamboyance? Seriously?

I never joke about flamingos. She tried to smile, but only wanted to be alone in her flat again now. She'd wash her hair, dry it before she slept. She'd fall asleep looking out on laundry-lined rooftops and palm trees from the window above her bed.

Nearly 50% of the bacteria in your body live on the surface of your tongue, offered Tom. Cathy had stuck out her tongue into the salty air.

I think that's true. And the human body contains three times more bacterial cells than human cells.

Is this a game? He'd smiled sideways at her.

Sure. She unclenched one fist, then the other, and tried to relax her shoulders.

The groove in the middle of the place above your lips is called a tragus.

False, that's this bit, Cathy touched the button of skin-covered cartilage on her ear. *The philtrum is above your lips.*

Tom shifted his lanky body, hesitantly, as if about to reach out and touch the groove above her lip, but then he didn't and they both looked away from each other. Cathy turned her head to check behind her and the men who had been staring were no longer there. She smiled with relief. Her heart was beating fast.

I didn't know that about flamingos, Tom said.

Cathy opened a low drawer of her cabinet, a childhood drawer, and picked up a toy lead soldier wearing a scuffed red jacket and a pointy black hat that shadowed his pinprick eyes. She put the lead soldier in the palm of her hand and wrapped her fingers around it. Small noises kept making her jump and her hands weren't steady enough to pin moths. She couldn't concentrate and even broke a wing, so had to stop. She was being awarded a prize that evening, for her research into the metamorphosis of hawkmoths, but would have to practise her speech later: she couldn't focus with the Kissing Beetle nearby.

She left the beetle in her cabinet but still had the lead soldier in her hand when, a few hours later, she walked out of the museum's wrought iron door into the humid Berlin sunshine. She thought it would be cooler out there under the museum's big birch tree than upstairs in her office with the chemicals and dust, but sweat continued to prick her skin. She sat down on a stone bench under the tree and put her thumb on the toy soldier's face.

The area outside the museum was busy with construction work. Cement mixers and diggers were everywhere that summer, stomping out the city's incidental monuments, turning its bullet-scarred buildings and graffiti-caked façades into boutique hotels and shopping malls. Great pink pipes snaked for miles, meandering past art galleries and building sites and directly in front of the museum, carrying water sucked out from under the city's surface. Perhaps it was because Berlin was built precariously on a marsh that Cathy felt so connected to the place. Below the pink pipes a girl in a denim skirt and a boy in board-shorts were eating sandwiches, while members of a gang of Japanese tourists were taking photos of each other. Sparrows were jumping around the lawn eating lunchbox crumbs; she tried not to watch the tight little shivers of their muscles. It was so hot that they burrowed their tummies in earth under the shrubs around the sandstone foundations of the building. A group of students were giving away flyers protesting against the museum being sponsored by the oil company. The protesters wore loose cotton trousers and tie-dyed skirts, their skin incandescent from conviction and sunshine.

Cathy typed 'Hotel Shiro' into Google on her phone. A map of central Berlin came up on the screen, with a red dot near *Alter Jüdischer Friedhof*, about twenty minutes' walk from the Natural History Museum. She knew that cemetery, she and Tom had walked through it a few times to see the ivy-covered stone angels. It was near a knotted junction of hotels and coffee shops at *Rosenthaler Platz* U-bahn, a mecca for coders bent over their Macs. She looked up and watched a few of the protesters sunbathing on the lawn outside the museum, taking a break to sit on the dried-out grass. One blonde teenager had her eyes closed and her claret-coloured mouth a little open, chin tilted to the sky as if drinking in the sunshine.

She pressed the 'call' button and rang Hotel Shiro.

"Good morning," said a voice on the phone. Cathy could hear the woman's fingers tapping on a keyboard and a baby crying. Cathy was sweating and had the impression that she could smell cottony laundry detergent and deodorant from under her arms, as well as stale sandwiches from kids eating lunch nearby. Whenever she was nervous, her sense of smell heightened.

"Do you have a Daniel Bower staying with you, please?"

More tapping. "Doesn't look like it. Have you got the right branch of Shiro? There is one in the centre of town."

A siren went off in the distance. Just to be sure, Cathy said: "How about Dan Green?"

The woman checked, fingernails clacking on the keyboard as she typed this name. "Yeah, shall I put you though?"

Cathy paused. For a moment, she felt as if something was stuck in her throat and that she wouldn't be able to speak, but then she heard herself say:

"Yes. Please."

The phone seemed to ring forever. She rubbed the angular limbs of her toy soldier between her fingers for comfort. Before the thirteenth ring, a raspy voice picked up:

"Hello?"

She recognised his voice. He sounded sleepy. Her body stiffened and a strong taste of acid, of vomit, arrived at the back of her mouth. She swallowed it back down again, a pattern of taste and revulsion that occurred repeatedly through the rest of that day. Almost immediately, more awake, he said: "Cathy?"

She fumbled and pressed 'end' on her phone as quickly as she could. She put the phone down. She wondered how he could have known it was her on the line.

A Seagull Skull

CATHY'S LUNGS HAD ached when she walked through the early morning darkness away from Daniel's sleeping body six years ago. It had been early and still dark when she ran. She'd carried her suitcase into St Osyth Town where the taxi was waiting for her. Her exit was meticulous because she'd planned it for months. *Angeles* was divine. *Los*, though, was loss.

She'd tried to call the police from a payphone outside The Red Lion Pub in town that morning but couldn't do it, because she could still sense the curves of his body against her skin and the smell of him in her hair. On arriving in Los Angeles she'd bought an international calling card from a liquor store called The Pink Elephant in East Hollywood and stood in the hot parking lot, staring at a phone booth littered with postcards of prostitutes. The sun had been so hot that the tarmac was sticky under her trainers and she felt as if the buttons on her skirt might melt.

She'd told the police everything she knew about Daniel, but standing there on the melting tarmac with her single suitcase, she'd missed the memory objects she'd been forced to leave behind in Essex. She had known she would not get away quickly enough while carrying suitcases full of sentimental driftwood and animal bones, so she'd transferred the edited version of her life into new shoeboxes she could take in her suitcase. Standing there in the Los Angeles car park, she'd felt a pang of longing for the dried flowers picked on dawn-time foraging missions with her father, and crayon drawings of birds she'd made while her parents argued. She missed the texture of her beloved orange rowing boat, which had fallen into pieces when she was fifteen, and her stuffed songbird with big plaintive eyes that she'd once loved to distraction but had now not dared to take through customs. Her fingers tingled at the thought of her seagull skeleton, which took months to clean and fit back together with wire and glue. She might have been free when she arrived in Los Angeles, but she was lonely without the tactile remains of her memories.

She wished that she could have brought her super colour 6355 camera to capture in pictures this new city. She would have taken a photo of the gritty motel on Hollywood Boulevard where she stayed her first week and the homeless man wearing a tutu who often sat by the stagnant pool. She loved Polaroids for their instant nostalgia, so accurate it made her heart ache. She brought one photo of Daniel with her to Los Angeles. He was knee deep in the estuary and grinning up at her with sparkling grey eyes. She was fascinated by how taking a photo somehow eradicated the actual moment. He had freckles and there was a bird circling above. Somehow, he looked like an animal, a natural part of the landscape around him rather than a human addition. She and Daniel had both been animal-like, then. She loved how photographs were not vulnerable to bias or emotions, how they were indifferent to hindsight.

She had left all her mother's hundreds of shoes in Essex. Her mother had wide feet and she was constantly on the search for *the perfect comfortable shoes*. She had worked in the shoe department of Debenhams before she married Cathy's father, then afterwards as a baker for the local café in St

Osyth. She was superstitious and would get genuinely upset if Cathy opened an umbrella in the house or walked underneath a ladder. She always smelt of lemon cake and Superking cigarettes and was constantly buying things that they couldn't afford, mostly shoes, trying to hide packages from Cathy's dad. It wasn't fetishist or extravagant: she just never seemed to own the right pair. She left Essex when Cathy was eleven years old and moved to Spain with a man she met at the café in town. Afterwards Cathy's father put the shoes in bin bags to rot in the cellar, but Cathy would go through them sometimes, observing how her mother's footprint was still in many of them, or droplets of her blood. It was basically a morgue of failed potential, all the people that her mother thought she might have been but wasn't. Cathy's favourites were a pair of wide-fit snakeskin kitten heels that, with all their straps, must have been ludicrously painful. Cathy also liked a pair of cork and plastic peep-toes she remembered her mother buying in Brighton and wearing just once, gleeful for about ten seconds before they started to rub her feet and she flung them grumpily into her handbag.

Cathy abandoned hundreds of Sea Roses and Yellow Horned Poppies in Essex when she ran away, dried specimens she'd found on the marsh during bird-watching sessions with her father before his liver gave up. If she had more of her objects perhaps she would remember her father better. She had to concentrate now in order to stop herself from thinking of him as a cartoon alcoholic who drank gin with his cornflakes and threw things, which is what he became. He used to have a big smile that showed a broken tooth at the side of his mouth and made the wrinkles on his cheeks bunch up into pleats. He used to be the king of finding unexpected bee species nesting on warm sunny ridges further away from the sea and he would speak of how his life mission had been conserving the nesting ground of Little Terns. There were literally thousands of feathers all over her father's house by the time he died, a few months before Cathy escaped Lee-Over-Sands. He died in a hospice, with five Brent Geese feathers in a vase by his bed instead of flowers.

In her cabinet she still had one of the dried tropical flowers with dagger-like orange petals that grew all over Los Angeles, on dusty street corners and around liquor store parking lots as well as in smart hotel driveways and gated Malibu mansions. She'd been surprised by how vicious this common flower looked when she arrived in her new city, and how unlikely. She had a little gold Buddha from a massage parlour and the flyer from a street puppet show she'd once stumbled on late at night while unable to sleep. She was in a constant half-awake state then, and spent nights walking through this new world, where she was free to do as she liked but had no idea what that was. She was lonely and collected objects from the city as she'd once collected them from the marsh: discarded shopping lists in spiral bound notepads, a skateboard wheel, a torn photograph of two lovers. Seemingly inanimate things have more power than most people wanted to accept. They can consume you or liberate you. They can drag you down for the rest of your life or, if you let them, take on the burden of remembering.

"Excuse me?" Cool fingers touched Cathy's warm arm and she flinched. She'd laid her head down in the palm of her hands after cancelling the call with Daniel, the lead soldier still in her hand, and now the Berlin daylight around her seemed unnaturally bright. She wasn't sure how long she'd been sitting like that. "Are you okay?" the voice said.

In front of her was the blonde protester with the claret coloured mouth who had been sunbathing a moment ago. Cathy forced herself to take a deep breath, to exhale slowly and smile. It had been hot like this the first summer she and Tom were in Berlin. They'd spent a month, both between jobs, listening to language tapes while wandering the city, occasionally stopping off at bars, monuments or man-made beaches by the Spree.

In front of the museum now, in the same heat as that first summer, the teenage protester's hair was cut straight across her shoulders and her forehead, a sharp fringe that almost obscured her eyes. She was tanned and radiantly confident, the sort to jump first when skinny-dipping in lakes with friends.

"I'm fine, thank you," Cathy said, composing herself and pushing her shoulders back. Through the museum's front doors Cathy could just hear the building's intercom telling everyone it was closing for a private function: they must have started to set up the party. Children trailed out of the front door, unwrapping melted chocolate bars and sucking on warm juice boxes.

"You flinch when you're touched," the teenager said to Cathy matter-of-factly. She must have been around seventeen, with thick eyelashes and a tattoo of a flower on her shoulder. "Do you feel tired, off balance?"

"I'm just hot," said Cathy. The girl made her think of fidgeting with half-wet candle wax between her thumb and forefinger. In another mood Cathy would have wanted to draw her into conversation. Cathy had always enjoyed talking to complete strangers. Not people at parties or friends of friends, but old women on the bus or loopy men in cafés. She'd get an urge to tell elderly couples in the park about how her father had once tried to suffocate the neighbour's tabby cat with a pillow because he thought it was murdering the nesting terns in the bird sanctuary, or confide in bartenders about how her mother used to sing Disney songs and show tunes while she cooked lemon cake. She didn't say anything to the protester.

"I wanted to give you this." The teenager pressed a flyer into Cathy's lap. It had a silhouetted picture of a dripping pelican against a white background. The pelican's beak drooled oil. "Smile cause it might never happen, you know." Cathy hated that phrase. People said it to her remarkably frequently. She saw that her hands were shaking. She wished she were in her noisy bed, asleep next to Tom. She wished she were sitting on *Kottbusser* Bridge with him, watching the canal underneath, or on a train zooming out of the city past rooftops and abandoned factories.

Cathy made her way back into the museum and paced down a long rubber-floored corridor. She couldn't face Tom for lunch because he'd know something was wrong.

With the soldier still in her fist she marched down a flight of stairs towards what was called the spirit collection. It was not a curated selection of souls, as the name suggested - nothing to do with the anatomy of phantoms or the evolutions of poltergeists - just rooms of specimens preserved in alcohol. There was air conditioning in the basement, one of the few temperature-controlled places in the museum. The cool air was relieving. Her breathing began to go back to almost normal, although her hands still shook. There was no phone reception down there, so neither Daniel or Tom would be able to call her. As she walked into the luminous corridors of the spirit collection, full of snakes and plants in fluid-filled jars, she imagined the markings on her skin from all the falls and slaps and bumps and fucks and hugs of her life so far, her physical existence sketched out as a topographical map with contour lines marking the terrain of her fingers, toes, tongue. The Essex mud flying up into her face when she stamped in it after the rain, sea holly scratching her ankles. Thumb marks on her wrists and bruises on her thighs, a map of all the places she'd left parts of her body, all the mouths and beds and cities and hotels and desks where she'd shed skin or blood or saliva. She hovered in the museum corridor and imagined her skin renewing itself, her cells transforming and growing over time until – as a molecular biologist would have it – there were none of the original cells left. None of the damage that Daniel had wrought.

A Raptor Claw

D ANIEL STOOD ABSOLUTELY still at his hotel
window after putting down the phone. The window
faced a nineteenth-century military cemetery, weeping grave
angels and wonky headstones just visible through sunlit trees.
On the street below, tourists and students drank coffee or
smoked cigarettes in the sunshine. Daniel had spent the previous day walking along the river Spree as it cut like a vein
through the centre, but he liked it best in his hotel room. Two
dreadlocked backpackers counted coins in their palms below
the window and a child licked an ice cream with an expression
of extreme, sullen concentration. How the child licked his
ice cream briefly made Daniel think of the jaunty ice-cream
vans and shark fossil shops in the town where he grew up, but
then he focussed back on his immediate surroundings. He
listened for noises in the corridor outside his room and in the
adjoining rooms. A conversation was going on in Japanese or
Chinese. A television in the next-door room droned with ads
for toothpaste and action movies.

Daniel's nose had a flat ridge down the middle and there
was a bump in his right cheek, which he noted as he stood,
dishevelled, looking into the mirror next to the window.
His body was larger than Cathy would have remembered,
with three tattoos on his arm that hadn't been there when
she'd known him. He pulsed his fists. As he reached to touch
the raptor claw on the desk and he thought of her perhaps

touching it later, both their fingers on the same surface, all the different moments that he'd known Cathy arrived simultaneously in his imagination. The young woman who disappeared in the middle of the night and thought she was free because she betrayed him. The sullen teenager with feverish skin who smelt of damp laundry and mud, collecting driftwood on the beach. The girl with a slack tomboy walk and a smile full of mockery. The child with matted bright orange hair cut short above her ears in a way that suggested she'd done it herself with kitchen scissors, whom he'd disliked immensely for her solitary and too-loud laugh, for the way she used to scream as she rode her bike over the seawall. She was still like a phantom limb: he had never quite stopped feeling her presence as an untouchable part of his body.

Amongst a million or so specimens hidden in the museum corridors and attics were seven entire elephants, sliced into pieces, along with three preserved gorillas, three twelve-foot whale skulls, two giraffes and four lions, their bodies all kept in vast fluid-filled tanks in ballroom-sized spaces. It was almost laughable. A scientist looking for a particular species often had to walk through miles of corridors to find what he or she was looking for.

On his way to the museum café for lunch with Cathy, Tom moved quickly past goats, rhesus monkeys and three-toed sloths, down the curled stairs towards the first floor landing. The museum was built on the site of an old ironworks factory, so banisters and cabinets all over the building curled with welded iron vines and animals. The entire east wing had been bombed at the end of World War II and never recovered from the second-floor insect collection exploding down into the first-floor library, which in turn landed in a tumble of beetle shells and reference books on top of a shattered beluga whale skeleton on the ground floor. The wing had been built up again slowly, like an expanding city, full of dead ends and circles.

"Don't touch the sun, please," said the guard to a child, ushering everyone out. This was the guard's main purpose in life, it seemed: to stop the sun getting sticky fingerprints on its surface. *He's creating an army of little Icaruses*, Cathy had noted once. Tom daringly touched the sun as he stepped out through the atrium.

The party was being set up and the smell of cut flowers hit him as he neared the hundreds of white roses and lilies spread across white fold-out tables, waiting to be arranged. Boxes of champagne flutes were being unpacked and ivory candles put into candelabras. Cardboard boxes were spilling over with papier mâché animal masks to be given out as party favours, each one fitted with black elastic to pull over the back of the head. Tom stopped to pick up a goat and a pig mask from the box, before putting them down again. Finally, he decided on a papier mâché bunny rabbit with a pink nose, white ears and a wistful expression on his face. He walked through the atrium carrying it.

"Berlin's Natural History Museum opens its doors tonight for its new gem gallery, 'All The Glitters'," a radio played. "Many of Europe's leading artists, donors and cultural supporters are expected to be greeted at the event. Also promising to make an appearance are members of an environmental group protesting against the museum's sponsorship by international oil conglomerate Global Petroleum."

Cathy wasn't in the café at their window table where they usually met for lunch, or outside under the tree where she sometimes sat in the shade. It was only ten past; he wasn't particularly late. He called her phone and it went straight to voicemail. She might have been on the line, but she often lurked down in the basement when it was too hot upstairs. There was no cell reception down there.

Down in the bowels of the museum a tall room was full of embalmed miniature dolphins, rat spines and forlorn sea-horses. Cathy was sitting at a metal counter on the far end, perched on a stool. The walls of specimen jars glowed around her with a yellow tint.

"Oh dear! Oh dear! I shall be too late!" He'd planned to say as he walked in the room with the rabbit mask on his face, pre-tending to be the White Rabbit in Alice in Wonderland. Only he caught a strange expression on her face before she realised he was there, which made Tom pause to observe her in silence for a moment before she saw him. When she didn't know he was looking at her, he would sometimes catch this feverish and uneasy glassiness on her pretty face. It used to happen a great deal when they first knew each other in Los Angeles, but had occurred less regularly once they moved to Berlin. It was a childish look and in those brief moments before she saw him and broke into a smile or a joke, she appeared lost. The expression would evaporate a second later, only visible when she thought he wasn't there.

Immediately on seeing him across the room, she reconfig-ured her expression into something more present.

"Hi," she smiled. "Did I forget about lunch? Sorry." She wasn't sorry. Her eyes remained bloodshot and her voice expressionless. Her skin was even whiter than usual now amongst the luminous jars of methylated spirit. She put her hand in her pocket, mock casual and boyish, but not quite pulling it off.

"Is something wrong?" he said.

"No," she smiled at him. It was a fake smile, though. The edges of her lips even shook slightly, objecting to being raised. Spontaneous and conscious smiles use completely different facial muscles. One is conjured up intentionally and the other is only partially a result of your known desires. Cathy's smile just then was a shop-assistant smile with blank eyes. She thought she was unreadable but she wasn't.

On the shelf behind her a stingray had its wings folded forward in an empty embrace inside a cylindrical tube, its own ludicrous grin visible on the flat underside of its body. She stepped back towards the chair again and as she did so, her elbow knocked over some of the glass specimen test tubes lined up on the desk. They both lunged to catch the test tubes as they rolled off. He saved one and the other slipped through her fingers to smash on the floor. The tubes were marked *Hyles gallii*, containing green caterpillars that were now limp squiggles on the floor. A smell of alcohol filled the air. Tom walked over and took her hands in his instead of letting her bend down and deflect her mood by picking up bits of glass and caterpillar from the floor.

"Is that one of the masks they're giving out at the party?" Cathy said, motioning the rabbit in his hand. Tom could see goose pimples on Cathy's neck and two creases in between her eyes. Perhaps Cathy was nervous about talking in front of so many people this evening when she received her prize.

"They have all sorts. Foxes, lions, pigs, zebras."

"Put it on then, White Rabbit." She took the mask from him and put it over his eyes, slipping the elastic tenderly behind his head.

"Everything okay?" he said.

"Oh, my paws and whiskers! I'll be late." She made her hands into paws and raised her eyebrows, putting on a rabbit-voice: "I'm late! I'm late! For a very important date!"

"Okay," said Tom, smiling. "You're okay."

"The Duchess! The Duchess! Oh my dear paws! Oh my fur and whiskers!"

Tom laughed and tucked her hair behind her ear, looking at her through the pinholes of his mask's eyes. "Why is a raven like a writing-desk?" he said.

"It's a poor sort of memory that only works backwards," she replied, and then paused. "Sorry to be jumpy. I think I'm nervous about this evening."

"Do you want to practise your acceptance speech?"

There was a sense of transience about Cathy, as if she might slip through Tom's fingers at any moment, disappear completely, or shape-shift. He could never quite put his finger on it, yet while her lips moved through her speech in the spirit collection and the blood came back to her face, Tom thought about how remarkable it was that it took months of being near Cathy even to realise she existed. She'd worked in the same museum as him in Los Angeles, but she was one of many mousy student scientists busy with minuscule and painstaking tasks. He may have once noticed her walking down Wilshire Boulevard in a prim shirt and ballet slippers and thought it a curious sight, because who on earth walks in Los Angeles, but he hadn't stopped to give her a ride. He would not have been able to describe her face or personality. At the time he was dating a surfing-obsessed blonde with anaesthetised big eyes that gave her a dopey expression; she was the sort of girl who touched her tank top straps and scratched her stomach in public. They used to have unsatisfying sex, self-consciously cinematic. He expected that she faked most of her orgasms and afterwards she always looked triumphant and despondent in equal measure.

Cathy was not his normal type by a long stretch. He spoke to her briefly during a Christmas party on Venice Beach once, more out of pity than anything else because she didn't seem to know anyone. The conversation had felt as if she were speaking the lines of a play, and she kept looking over her shoulder, distracted. The second time he saw her was after he broke up with his surfer girlfriend and spent the night at some other similarly blonde and tanned woman's run-down apartment in La Brea, not far from the museum. Madly hung-over, he'd stumbled into his one-night-stand's bathroom and moved a hand down to his pyjama bottoms to piss. He'd heard a noise to his right so glanced blearily towards the tub, where the girl from the Christmas party was lying naked in water the colour of the avocado bathroom tiles. She had a scar on her forehead that he hadn't noticed on the beach. Her breasts and one knee made islands above the water while most of her body was a subterraneous landscape. Her nipples were larger than he would have expected, and almost the colour of bruises. Her hair was a similar colour, dark from the bathwater and spread out around her shoulders. One of her ankles hung over the edge of the bath. She didn't cover her body but raised a single eyebrow at him. His hand was still on his half-hard morning cock and she laughed. When her face crinkled he noticed her knuckle-pale cheekbones and how her eyes were blue rather than brown, which he never would have guessed.

There was something about her laugh that morning and the glint in her eyes that took his breath away. She'd materialised in front of him, a ghost stepping from an empty space. There was a stillness about her that made him want to be near her. He tried to sketch her body from memory later that day, but found it impossible to capture the shape of her eyelids, how her second toe was marginally longer than her big toe, or the shape of her lips when she frowned. It turned out that even photographs never really looked like her at all. He started to sketch her and leave his drawings on her desk, which he hoped wasn't creepy but probably was; he teased her, became fascinated by her secretive smile, and asked her out so many times she eventually said yes. Later, he moved half way around the world because she wanted to explore the world. Everyone thought he was crazy, but from that moment in the bath he'd been devoted.

The Calla Lily Inn was off-season and almost empty; the only other guests were four elderly women having their yearly get-together, cackling by the pool and chain-smoking Virginia Slims. Cathy hadn't told anyone that she and Tom would be staying in Palm Springs, an hour's drive from Los Angeles. They had spent that week reading science journals and playing cards on glass topped tables by the pool, he lounging in the sun while she read in the shade with her head resting on fraying patio cushions, surrounded by palm and banana trees. Surfacing from the hotel each evening, smelling of chlorine and sex, they went for hamburgers on Canyon Way or to the cinema on Calle Alvarado. There was a wig shop next to the cinema and one night they spent hours choosing between blonde synthetic bobs and curly black ones that transformed her face. In a feathered blonde hairstyle her eyes looked different, less blue but larger. Shoulder length waves made her cheekbones stand out. It was a curiosity of Cathy's adolescence that her frizzy orange hair had turned much darker around the time she started getting breasts and hips and bleeding. It had darkened so much that people who knew her as a kid didn't necessarily recognise her. The wig styles in Palm Springs had names such as 'Applause', 'Envy' and 'Snuggle'. Tom bought her a black one called 'Nocturnal' that made her skin ghostly. She wore it all evening and was amazed how people stared and men smiled. People did not usually notice her from a distance; her appeal was a close-quarters thing. She was still wearing it when they returned to the hotel.

While Tom stripped off his T-shirt and glasses to dive straight into the swimming pool the innkeeper handed Cathy their room key and a small parcel. She held her breath and opened the parcel before Tom got out of the pool, fumbling through tissue paper. Inside was an inch-long fossilized tooth that she took out and held between her fingers.

What's that you got there, honey? The manager looked a bit worried.

An alligator tooth, I think. Cathy continued to hold it and studied its sharp tip. She slipped the black wig off her head, abruptly self-conscious, turning around to see if anyone was watching her. Assuming Daniel had gone to prison, and she had to assume that, then he would have been inside for over a year by then. He had friends, though. Behind her she could only see shaky desert air and tropical flowers, but decided she would make an excuse to go back to Los Angeles the next day. This was worse than him just knowing where she lived.

Lord, for a minute I thought it was a bullet. A bullet in the mail! It did have the shape and weight of a bullet, Cathy thought. Glossy black and brown enamel. *Oddly enough, I've had a guest receive bullets in the mail before, but a pack of them. You see all sorts in my line of work. But never known someone get a tooth.*

No, said Cathy. *Not a bullet.* The next day she slipped off into town, saying she was going to an art gallery and instead went to an Internet café to shut down her email account, then persuaded Tom that they should go home earlier than planned. She'd had four email accounts and three phone numbers since leaving him, just in case that was how he was finding out where she was all the time. For the fifth time since arriving in Los Angeles, she moved apartments again. It didn't ever make a difference. In cinema queues and buses she would think she saw one of Daniel's friends, half-remembered faces from her past, and a moment later whoever it was would be gone.

A pinch of good quality grave dirt and some 1000-year-old hair, you got yourself a Voodoo curse. The innkeeper had grinned with big crimson lips. *I'm kidding, honey. You've gone even whiter than you looked in that wig.*

It's someone reminding me they're thinking of me.

They could have sent a greetings card.

Cathy had smiled without enthusiasm.

As the sun cooled down Daniel made his way steadily through Berlin towards the museum with the sea eagle claw in the pocket of his suit. "Across Europe this week the heat wave has caused wheat crops to burn," said an English paper in a newsagent's, "while strawberries have been left to rot because they cannot be picked fast enough". Daniel bought the newspaper and flicked through the pages before dumping it in a rubbish bin as he turned onto a main road. His shoes rubbed and he knew that his white shirt would be sweaty by the time he arrived. A baby screamed from under a ridiculous white sun hat and an old man stood out on the pavement to smoke, wiping his brow. Crowds poured out of *Nordbahnhof* station, many of them talking on their phones. He had a sense that he was made of a far heavier substance than everyone else on the streets and that people noticed the encumbrance apparent in each of his movements. He sensed people gave him a wide birth on the hot pavement.

Nearer the museum some streets were being dug-up. A smell of melted tarmac hit his nostrils as diggers lurched their necks, little Hitachis and giant yellow CATs both biting at the road. Daniel observed leathery men bending and shouting amongst their metal animals. The men reminded him of his father, as did the smell of tar and aggregate being pressed down by a steamroller. He could almost see his mother waiting on the sidelines to give his dad his sandwich and thermos at lunchtime. Daniel hadn't spoken to either of his parents in years, although they still lived in the same suburban Chelmsford house he and his brother Jack had been brought up in, with the same frosted glass door and lace curtains. Daniel had stopped by their house to watch them just before he came to Berlin and almost not recognized the two old people returning from the weekly supermarket shop on a Friday afternoon. They were bent and chalky-haired. The last time he'd seen them they'd been substantial and angry people. Daniel had wanted to knock on the door but hadn't been able to bring himself to do it. He wasn't sure what they knew of his life now. He'd wanted to cross the road and help his father with the shopping but couldn't.

Back when Daniel and his younger brother still lived with his parents in that house with lace curtains and a frosted glass door, Daniel had worked for a construction company. It was not the same one as his father worked for, but run by a man named Marcus who also owned a nightclub, a garage and a fleet of lorries. Daniel had spent a month the winter before his nineteenth birthday re-cladding and decking a chalet out on a desolate stretch of marshland called Lee-Over-Sands. Each of the twelve shacks appeared to be made out of driftwood. They had flat asphalt roofs and no water mains, just plastic butts outside. The chalets were perched on cinder blocks to protect them from flooding but still their walls were sodden. Ragged electricity cables looped down the street, blackbirds sitting on them. Sometimes the birds bounced on the wires as if for the fun of throwing out sparks in bright patterns. Daniel later discovered these birds could cause fires in the fields behind the houses. *Little pyromaniacs*, Cathy's father once described them.

Daniel had liked the military defence pill boxes on the estuary left over from World War II, giant moss-covered stepping stones lined up to stop the tanks rolling inland. The marshland area was transformed from a military defence to an industrial lot for making gravel after the war. Then in the

Fifties the holiday cottages were built and the gravel pit turned into a bird sanctuary that filled the space between the estuary and the beach to the right of the houses. At low tide you could wade right out of the houses over the estuary and the marsh and it took just ten minutes to reach the beach. At high tide it would take twenty minutes because you had to go over a rickety bridge and through the bird sanctuary.

It looks like a fucking ugly alien planet, the painter on that job had said.

Daniel loved the alien landscape but did not say so. When the tide changed, sucking and pushing, it confused your sense of gravity. The liquid had different textures, depending on whether the tide was coming in or going out. Daniel began arriving early at the site and leaving late so he could walk on the beach at different times of day. Across the water was a small town with two turrets on its peninsular, an aging nuclear power station that sat on the horizon like a lost toy. During breaks from pounding nails and cutting wood Daniel would walk over to the second house from the end, which had a repossession sign in one of its windows.

Daniel had been a carpenter for three years by then and had saved some money. He'd won a few amateur boxing matches and lived with his parents, so he hardly spent anything. He wanted to get started on his life, and didn't give much thought to the risk of borrowing money from his boss. Daniel's father thought he was getting ahead of himself and that the area was a dump, built quite literally on a sinking coastline at the edge of a marsh. His dad was a tentative man who never went on holiday or took a day off work. He thought buying the chalet would be a dubious investment, but Daniel badly wanted to own it, to transform it into a shabby-chic weekend retreat for London types and make a profit. The deck on the repossessed house was half fallen down, covered in rusted metal and fishing nets. Peeking through gaps in the boarded-up windows, he could see that the floorboards were warped and the doors hanging off their hinges. An ancient deck chair was upturned in the middle of the living room. Daniel thought he'd put in a second level with glass windows to let in the sun. He imagined he and Jack would spend weekends together crabbing off the deck, watching football in the living room, taking a boat down the estuary, having barbecues as the sun went down over the sea. Jack was nine years old then, a geeky and shy kid whom Daniel adored.

Only one of the chalets was inhabited that first winter, the one at the estuary's curve, where a middle aged ginger-haired man spent most of his days wrapped in blankets, bird watching on the deck and sipping whiskey straight from the bottle. The man's face was lean, with broken capillaries all over his nose and cheeks.

The seagulls are laughing at us! The drunk had said once, when he saw Daniel peering into the window of the derelict chalet next door. The seagulls were, indeed, giggling. The soundtrack to life on the wrong side of the seawall was provided by these hysterical seagulls.

Most beautiful place in the world! The drunk shouted against the wind. Daniel agreed. He noticed that a ginger-haired child appeared occasionally at the chalet window or running over the marshes as if she were being chased. She wasn't in focus for him then, she was just the daughter of a drunk who lived nearby. Daniel had wondered if Jack would make friends with her when he visited for weekends. Daniel remembered flashes of a kid's Wellington boots splashing desperately through the mud, a knot of red hair in the distance, a grazed knee running through the marsh, a vague sense of unease, even then, at the sight of her.

A Lion Mask

CATHY'S EVENING DRESS hung next to Tom's tuxedo, both in dry-cleaning bags full of the deflated people they were about to become. She'd put their clothes here a few days ago, away from the smell of naphthalene and ethanol that haunted the other floors of the museum. Cathy untangled her dress from its static plastic and stripped off her white shirt and bra, her grey trousers and ballet shoes. She stood naked in front of Tom for a moment with the stone floor cold under her bare feet, surrounded by bones.

"Should we get married in the museum?" she said.

"The stuffed polar bear can be ring *bearer*," Tom smiled. "Sorry."

"Ba-ba-boom," Cathy smiled at his crap joke.

Everyone called this room bone cellar. It housed dinosaur vertebrae the size of tractor wheels and mammoth thigh bones that could not easily be transported. Each of the objects was scrawled upon with the name of the quarry from which it had been dug while the museum's collection number was usually printed more neatly on a fracture. Tom pressed the centre of his broken glasses higher up the ridge of his nose with his index finger. He still had the rabbit mask perched on top of his head. It was cool in the room.

She took her green dress off its hanger. She'd bought it from *Mauerpark* flea market the previous week. They'd gone to the market together, perusing East German family photo albums and dolls with knotted hair while buskers beat their drums and played the saxophone in the park beyond. When she got the dress home she found moth holes in the lining, which made her laugh because moths were her area of expertise. Her PhD thesis had been an investigation into the long-held assumption that during a moth's metamorphosis the caterpillars literally digest their own bodies, liquefying themselves almost completely until only cells called 'imaginal cells' survived, blueprints so distinct from the caterpillar that its immune system tries to kill them. She liked that idea but didn't believe it. Her work had revolved around training caterpillars to avoid certain odours that were associated with a mild shock and discovering that the adult moths continued to avoid these smells after metamorphosis. Cathy had proved that along with these prettily-named imaginal cells, memory-storing neurons must survive the digestion process to become incorporated into the moth's brain. Childhood was crouched inside the moth, just like the human.

"What's a rabbit's favourite music?" Tom said. Cathy shrugged and Tom ran a finger down her torso from her collarbone all the way to her hip. She often felt a kind of shock when observing that she was indisputably an adult now, baffled by the finality of her limbs and the increasing permanence of each decision she made with them.

"Hip hop," Tom answered himself and laughed at his own joke. She laughed too, mostly because he was laughing. "What are you thinking about?" he said.

"Rabbits?" What Tom would most like to do was to take her apart and observe all her crevices and connections, and then fit her together again. He grew up with a big family of tanned blonde sisters and stepbrothers in a rambling house by Griffith Park in East Hollywood. His father was a heart surgeon and his mother was a screenwriter, both gregarious people who persuaded Cathy to do things like join family soft-ball teams and play board games after dinner. She always felt oddly lonely when his family were nearby, although they were wonderful. It was so different from her family. Elevator doors never closed on Tom, puddles didn't splash him and airlines never lost his luggage. His parents had told him he was lucky so many times that by the age of ten when he cut out coupons from cereal packets or newspapers and didn't get sent the gift basket, he assumed there had been a bureaucratic mistake. He said that over the course of his competition-entering child-hood, he'd won family tickets to Universal Studios, a crate of sparkling wine, a lifetime supply of Hershey's Kisses (which turned out to be fifty boxes), a $600 television, a limited edition box set of *The Godfather* and a camping lantern. He had the confidence of a person who had been loved a great deal, unconditionally, when growing up.

She'd wanted Tom from the first time they spoke in Venice Beach. He had an easy nonchalance and even his outlandish character-traits, such as how he told terrible jokes and was fascinated with Tarot cards, seemed enviably normal. She would watch him flirt with interns and tourists out in the sunshine or in the staff rooms, laying down Tarot cards for them. *Death,* she'd overheard him saying, mock-solemnly, his mouth frowning and inquisitive eyes smiling with pleasure at the drama of it all, *but that's ok. Death is change. Change is good; it's what we're all searching for.* She'd overheard girls saying they believed he really was psychic. She told herself she would never allow Tom to read her fortune. *The Fool,* she imagined him saying to girls.

It wasn't difficult to get his attention when she decided to. He seemed confused by his feelings for her, but that didn't matter. They smiled at each other over staff meetings, ate pizza after work, and he left sketches for her on her desk. Eventually, when she took off her clothes for him in his studio loft a few blocks from the museum, there were Tarot cards strewn over the bed. The Sun. The World. The Hermit. He thought he'd charmed her, but it was Cathy who'd won. He assumed he'd waged war on her remoteness but she'd told him next to nothing of her life. His skin smelt of dirt and, somehow, sunlight. He did not guess that she'd grown up in a place that smelt of sewage, stealing lunch money from her dad's pocket when he was passed out, and never having friends over. He did not guess that she had learnt to keep her memories trapped inside objects, where mercurial things could be archived and controlled. He did not realise that she spent her life being told she was bad.

There was dust in Tom's facial stubble and his bushy eyebrows, thousand-year-old specks that had been eased from a mammoth tibia with a dental pick and camel hairbrush. He always had dirt under his bitten-down fingernails. She'd spent the day cataloguing microscopic wings and antennae, using a needle to excavate the inner matrices of abdomens and thoraxes. She'd taken off his glasses and kissed his warm mouth, moving her hands down under his belt.

She had to stop herself from acting like it was as much a fight as a fuck, which was how sex had always been before Tom. She'd only slept with two men before. She lost her virginity in one of the bird watching huts on the marshes, aged fifteen, to a gypsy boy whose mouth tasted of the seafood restaurant where he worked. She'd bit the boy's lip and he bled more than she did. Then, aged nineteen, there had been Daniel, with whom pain was the norm. Tom was different from both. She'd taken Tom's glasses off and kissed his warm mouth. The love was so different from anything she'd felt before. She did not feel she was merging with him, but that she became a more complete person in his presence. She was larva wriggling from her chrysalis then; she was turning into something new and she loved him for the freedom she felt in his presence. From that moment with Tom on the floor of his apartment her nightmares became a little less regular. She did not wake up five times a night any more, hearing the squall of seagulls and thinking she'd been knocked unconscious. Her dreams of choking, or drowning, became less intense, and often if she slept in the crook of his arm she didn't dream at all.

She never lied to Tom, exactly; she just never told him the entire truth. She did not want him to know of the person she'd been before she met him. A man like Tom never would have fallen in love with a girl like the Cathy of Lee-Over-Sands. His girlfriends had names like Arbela and Cynthia, with long tanned legs and weekly tennis lessons. Being with Tom made her past feel untraceable and she liked that feeling. She wanted him to always love her like he did that first night and never be disappointed in her, or disgusted by things she had done before she knew him.

The air was still warm as Daniel merged with other guests walking on a red carpet towards the museum's ornate iron door. Crowd barriers straddled either side of the pathway, with photographers lurking behind them along with five absurd-looking protesters wearing swimming costumes, their skin covered in some glossy black substance. It was supposed to look like petroleum; maybe it was body paint or food dye. Two of the activists held up signs with photographs of pelicans covered in oil. There had been an oil spill off the coast of Denmark recently and thousands of birds had died. The protesters shouted out 'Slick PR Won't Cover Your Spill!' as guests walked into the museum. Daniel stretched his aching fingers. The sea eagle claw weighed down one of his suit pockets.

The tuxedo-clad doormen kept glancing up at the semi-naked protesters, distracted from their jobs collecting invitations. Daniel stepped easily into the party at the elbow of an elderly woman with long grey hair and a velvet ball gown. Nobody asked Daniel to show his invitation. Despite feeling as if he'd just been untethered, that people avoided him in the street now, he walked easily into the party. The throng of people moved forward. Nobody told him that he was out of place amongst guests with smooth hands who wore velvet and smiles and gems. A waiter offered him champagne while a waitress handed him a papier-mâché lion eye mask with an elastic loop to go around his head. The mask had big eyes and varnished orange skin. He put it on, covering the top of his face.

A woman wearing a papier-mâché zebra held her skirt hems off the ground in the marble-floored entrance hall and a man wearing a toucan did up his shoelaces. Daniel almost expected Cathy to appear immediately in front of him. Instead there were dinosaurs strung like puppets surrounded by pigs with exaggerated eyelashes and owls with little black beaks. The neck of the tallest dinosaur nearly reached the room's triangulated glass ceiling. The heart of the Brachiosaurus, a sign said underneath it, would have weighed 400kg, as much as a horse. Other, smaller, dinosaurs ran alongside the giant, in between all these people.

Daniel continued through the party, uncomfortable in his suit. He didn't like crowds. At the back of the atrium a four-person jazz band was playing next to a 150-million-year-old bird trapped in Bavarian limestone. It was a lizard with wings, a link between dinosaurs and birds, according to the sign. The creature appeared to have been dancing with wild abandon, arms flung up in a chaos of pleasure before getting squashed mid-pirouette. He had come to the museum yesterday to give her the Kissing Beetle, thinking he would wait for her outside, but then he saw a van unloading party supplies into the museum's side door. A red carpet had lolled from the back of the van like a tongue and there was a sign above the door wishing the museum a happy 150th birthday.

The air was sludgy and too hot. He scanned the crowd for Cathy. She might not even be there. She wasn't a huge fan of parties. Guests were taking photos of themselves with the open-mouthed seven-foot polar bear at the back of the room, while a giraffe head jutted out from the wall amongst deer and leopards. If Cathy were with him she'd describe their characters: there was no such thing as an inanimate object in her book. These would be eager bulls, a flirtatious giraffe, a dubious fox. She was always 'doing the voices' of objects, even after she'd grown up. Sunglasses would often have conversations with muddy boots in the chalet they used to share on the coast; her fragments of strangely shaped driftwood would discuss the weather. He thought of white sheets and Cathy's body tangled up in them, all nearly the same morning-white-light colour, her body and the cotton.

Daniel turned towards the gems, where more guests were lingering and chatting along the left hand side of the room. In high-tech cabinets of spot-lit rocks, Serbian Jadeite was displayed next to a Martian meteorite that had fallen near Tissint in Morocco in July 2011. He caught sight of his face in a mirror behind the meteorite and almost didn't recognise himself in his suit. He hadn't been clean-shaven in years. He could easily pass in the crowd, he thought, surprised, although the semi-circles under his eyes resembled three-day-old bruises. The roots of his curly hair had flecks of grey in its black coils now. The skin was lined around his eyes and mouth.

At the far end of the atrium he could see a sliver of daylight through the front door and he wished he were out there in the fresh air instead of in this stifling gallery of gems and dead bones. He badly wanted to be alone again, far away from all these people, back in the safety and control of his hotel room. He told himself he was just here to see a girl who had done a great deal of harm to him in his life, to give her a gift in person, to scratch a perfectly reasonable itch, to know what her voice sounded like now, what expression her eyes would have when she saw him again.

Cathy stood on the balcony that circled the atrium and watched the party fill up below her. The museum no longer smelt of bones and children but like a smart department store. Tom was speaking to some of the museum's donors below her. He appeared schoolboy-ish in anything that wasn't made to measure, a teenager in the midst of a growth spurt. He was an excellent networker, though, always speaking to the right people and smiling at their jokes. Cathy stared around the atrium at all its obvious wealth and the shoes without scuff marks. Each person was two-faced, with their animal masks on their faces or heads. There were maybe five hundred guests in the atrium and adjoining galleries, all speaking above music that echoed in a tall space built exclusively for museum hush. The sound of protesters on the lawn outside was mostly drowned out by the jazz band and close-packed conversation, but between songs Cathy heard chanting. She hardly knew anyone in the room, and even the ones she did know looked like strangers tonight. She pretended to herself that she wasn't scanning the room for Daniel. He'd always hated crowds and she'd never seen him at a party before, certainly not one like this.

A television newsreader was holding court below her. Cathy visualised the guy without skin or three-piece suit, his skeleton arranged on a varnished wood block. The women he was surrounded by would be presented alongside like gazelles at a watering hole. These guests were the current victors on this planet, eating canapés around the naked bones of species that had been remiss enough to allow their extinction. So the humans peered at their ancient predecessors, gossiped over fossilised bones, magnanimously considered buying raffle tickets to support the museum's upkeep. Cathy hoped that one day another species would create new museums and amble around staring at human spinal columns and fossilised toes.

Cathy stiffened and cocked her head to the side, listening to her heartbeat. She could feel it under her tongue and in her neck. She'd been right about the voice on the phone: Daniel was there in the crowd, a stone's throw away across the room. He wasn't supposed to be out for another year. The last four years had lulled her into a false sense of security: she'd honestly thought he might have forgotten about her. His curly hair was sticking out of a lion mask as he read signs around the side of the room without speaking to anyone. She recognised the slope of his shoulders. His mask was bright yellow with serrated orange edges that were supposed to resemble a mane, but made her think of sunrays. Underneath the lion's head was a square jaw covered in waxen skin and that thin, tight mouth. He was a suit amongst other suits and tuxedos. He was sipping champagne just like everyone else in the room. Blood rose to the surface of Cathy's skin. She actually felt her veins plump up, acutely aware of her body.

She'd seen his face in this hallucinogenic way before – a sketchy, severed portion of a man's profile in a car during a traffic jam, or an incorrectly recognized frown in the cinema before lights went down. Even a smell could sometimes make her think he was nearby, a man passing by in a crowd who had created some invisible chemical reaction in her body, a misreading of pheromones, a tangle of chemical messengers creating spontaneous and undesirable images: her mouth licking the curve of his neck in the salty air, the angle of his smile. It had always turned out not to be him, of course.

Daniel lifted the mask briefly and turned his head. Her blood was rushing, a panic of activity that made her fingers tingle and her shoulder tense. Cathy took a step backwards from the balcony so he wouldn't see her. His eyes appeared momentarily from under the mask. His clean-shaven jaw emphasised his large, flat-ridged nose that didn't exactly match the nose in her memory. His eyebrows were bushier than she remembered. It was peculiar to see him with such distance, without touch or smell and after this gap in time. Then someone stepped in front of him and the crowds shifted so she only saw flashes of him between heads and shoulders, just fragments of his nose or hands or shoulders.

There was too much saliva in her mouth, and her armpits dampened. She wiggled her toes in her uncomfortable shoes and the area between each toe was wet as well. Her tongue rested in the gap on the bottom row of her teeth where she was missing a molar. The gap began to throb as if it recognized Daniel's presence in the room. A bone in her right foot that never healed correctly ached and the far right edge of her collarbone seemed to twitch where once it had been fractured. Humans have twenty-seven bones in their hands. Gorillas have thirty-two. Such a complicated mesh of bones meant that if you fracture your scaphoid it will never heal quite right. You have a map of every break in your fingers forever, as she did, along with the map of scars on her skin. She tasted vomit in her mouth again and swallowed it down. She'd put the lead toy soldier in her handbag earlier. Now she took it out to hold in her fist.

Having Tom and Daniel in the same space was as if two rebel versions of her soul had broken free of her body and were about to meet without her having the slightest bit of control over the result. Daniel was the most solid thing in the room. It had always been the case that wherever he stood, whether it was on a building site or in an antique shop or on the beach, he appeared to put down roots. He belonged wherever he happened to be standing. Daniel put the lion mask back down over his eyes and turned away again. Around him young women flicked their hair and men were led around by their ample stomachs. Pearls and hairspray glinted. Museum curators and technicians laughed loudly, betraying nasal problems and bad teeth.

At the far end of the atrium the jazz band briefly paused and the thunder of conversation became louder, but then the music started up again and drowned it out. Feet danced in time with a saxophonist's hands and a bow sliced at double bass strings. Lions discussed their careers with foxes. Cathy thought back to how, as her relationship with Daniel was ending and she had become terrified of him, they had sat together on her porch at low tide with their toes in the mud. Daniel's friends had been in the chalet that day, with their lopsided lorry-driver tans and wrist watches they shouldn't have been able to afford.

Do you remember how you and Jack would make mud men down there at low tide, with carrots for noses just like snowman? Daniel had squeezed her hand.

Sure, she'd said. He'd always had the knack of making her feel scared and safe simultaneously, as if he was both the enemy and the only person who could save her.

A Pinned Butterfly

TOM SMOKED ON the steps outside the museum and idly watched the half-naked protesters beyond. Floodlights illuminated the building's façade. "End Oil Sponsorship!" they occasionally shouted, their shiny darkened faces intense. Immaculately dressed party guests smoked outside the museum's wrought-iron doors. A bearded man lit an old woman's cigarette and she smiled shyly. The smokers concentrated on ignoring the chanting.

"Are they covered in treacle, do you think?" Tom heard a smoker say. Tom tilted his head to the side. He wondered if Cathy had seen the protesters. He stared out onto the road beyond the museum's front lawn where an actress in a shimmery dress stepped from a limo and began walking towards the party. Tom recognised the actress from billboards and horror movies. She had the ideal face of a doll and was with an older man. The actress made Tom momentarily nostalgic for Los Angeles, for palm trees and swimming pools. He loved his life in Berlin but missed his parents and their backyard in East Hollywood, full of car engine parts and honeysuckle. His mother had a knack for attracting strays and their Thanksgiving lunches were legendary, attended by a constantly expanding crew of stunt doubles and insurance salesmen, minor celebrities and academics.

As the couple walked arm in arm towards the museum

entrance, some of the protesters reached behind some bushes and then quickly appeared again, ready for their big finalé. It happened quickly. A bodyguard emerged from nowhere to launch at the protesters, but by then the sticky content of the buckets had been lobbed in the direction of the red carpet where the actress and her date turned away a moment too late. They were immediately covered in thick black muck. The two guests hurtled back towards their limo, dripping. The police must have been waiting just beyond the lawn because they appeared on the scene almost immediately.

"Don't let Global Petroleum clean up their image without cleaning up their oil!" the protesters shouted. A few photographers had stayed outside and their cameras flashed now while the dripping older man helped his grimacing yet still beautiful lady climb back into her seat. The actress may have been crying, bitterly regretting having accepted an invitation from the PR Director of Global Petroleum. A male protester with a Mohawk hairstyle grabbed his backpack from behind a bush at the edge of the lawn and ran off down the street, a half-naked punk shimmering in the darkness. Tom wished Cathy were there to laugh about it with him. Two of the other protesters were bundled into a police car. The moon was fat and high in the sky, surrounded by faint streaks of cloud, and allowed Tom to see that one of the female protesters had run around the side of the museum before the policemen could grab her. Tom stayed and smoked in the warm evening for a little while longer.

Jonas the guard was not guarding the solar system as he ought to have been, but was instead craning his neck to catch a glimpse of the commotion outside the museum. Cathy couldn't see Tom in the party just then; she knew he was probably smoking outside on the steps. She didn't think that Daniel had seen her yet. He'd hovered almost casually at the edges of the party for a while, drinking champagne and apparently studying dinosaur eggs and Trilobites, then moved off towards the back of the atrium.

As she readied herself to face him, making her way through the animal bodies, she would have liked to press pause so she could scan the party for all its minute detail - observe puckering skin under the chins of elderly women, dirt forgotten at the edges of fingernails - but instead she drank a glass of champagne in one gulp. She didn't usually drink, because her father was an alcoholic and she quite liked the stuff as well. She weaved between foxes and zebras, unhooking the velvet rope to step into the solar system. She squinted through a wooden archway to the right of Pluto, into a dark connecting room with panelled ceilings and dioramas of animals poised in stage-set natural habitats. She expected Daniel to be loitering in front of the grizzly bears. He always used to like dioramas. Light twitched underneath drawn curtains, faintly illuminating an eagle nesting inside a cave of rocks in which a technician had left a stepladder and a can of paint, ruining the effect. Cathy saw that the room was empty, but she heard a creak of movement above her. She ought to have turned back then, before it had even started.

Instead she drifted up the stairs, the fingers of her right hand sweaty on the cast-iron banister and the fingers of her left sweaty around the toy soldier. She was an adult now; she could face him. The hairs on her neck and hands pricked as she crooked her neck to look up. Daniel was standing on the first floor landing with his elbows leaning on the balcony, his thin lips smiling down at her under his lion eye mask. She opened her mouth to speak but instead held tight to the toy soldier. Daniel jolted his head backwards, motioning for her to come upstairs, then shrank back into the shadows. She bent to unhook her sandals and walked up barefoot.

The previous week, before coming to Berlin, Daniel had made his way back to Lee-Over-Sands. He'd caught the train to Clacton-On-Sea and walked for two hours until he reached Lee-Over-Sands. The lorry company's garage was now a Tesco Metro. He'd walked by without stopping into the town nearest to his chalet, St Osyth. There were new restaurants on the main street, the teashop had become an Indian restaurant, and a gift shop had turned into a KFC. Over the sea wall and past the sewage plant, he'd trudged towards Lee-Over-Sands and had found all the chalets there bustling with families and warm lights. Cathy's old chalet had been torn down and they were building something vast and modern in its place. Around the back, some old wood, which may have been the cladding of the previous house, was piled up and in the process of being burnt. Daniel looked through the windows and saw architect diagrams pinned on the walls and marsh water seeping up through the floor. Daniel had stood in front of his old chalet, which was newly painted with a fresh asphalt roof. He could smell cooking, maybe a roast chicken, and hear laughter. Through the window a family was eating dinner together in a small kitchen. They'd built a sunroof up top, as Daniel had once planned to do. He must have stood there for longer than he should have, because a man in a polo shirt came out the front door and put his hands on his hips.

Can I help you? the man had said. He squinted at Daniel, who knew his eyes were sunken and his hair probably wild. Inside, the man's family had stopped eating and were glancing shiftily out of the window.

I used to live here, Daniel replied. *I was wondering if I could come and look around?* Daniel didn't mean any harm. He'd just come to see the place in which the most important events of his life had taken place.

It's late, the man said. *I'm sorry, but we're eating dinner.*

It will only take a minute.

I'd like you to leave now, the man said.

I'm on public property.

You're making my family uncomfortable.

I'd just like to see my old house.

I will call the police.

Why would you do that? Daniel wondered if they knew who he was, and what had happened in the chalet. *You don't need to do that,* Daniel said, and turned away. *I'm leaving.*

He'd slept in one of the bird watching huts that night, in the strange absolute blackness of the marsh. He'd dreamed of Cathy's tights low between her crotch because they'd shrunk in the wash. He'd dreamed of her licking her dry lips as a child. Cathy, nineteen, still with knees and ribs as bony as bird-skulls, sitting naked and cross-legged on the deck working on a tan that never came. He used to drop her off at lectures outside some sixties concrete block of Essex University and feel fiercely protective as she marched boyishly into the building, the cool kids all looking at her like she was feral. That night in the bird hut he dreamed about the unique blue colour of her eyes and how her face would go liquid when she drank too much.

He allowed himself to think what it would be like if she were to come back with him to Lee-Over-Sands. They would rent one of the chalets. Perhaps they would cook hamburgers out on the deck, covering them in a vast amount of ketchup. She would laughingly make him wear oven mitts to bed again, so he didn't scratch his eczema during the night. He would watch her out on the marsh in her nightgown on summer evenings, catching moths with a butterfly net. She used to set up a torch on some dry bit of the marsh and for an hour or so would attract swarms of them to her body. She'd put her hostages in specially made jam jars, each with a little bit of poison at the bottom, and by morning every spare surface of their flat would be full of asphyxiated creatures. *They don't know they're dying, isn't it great?* She used to say, getting ready to pin them.

After waking up in the bird hut he walked to an Internet café in Clacton. It wasn't difficult to work out where she was now. He'd lost track of her over the last four years, hadn't been able to send her gifts because Marcus and the rest of the haulage company had been arrested by then. On the web he saw that she'd been interviewed about her research in a journal called The Annual Review of Entomology and had an article published in a journal called Systematic Entomology. Both referenced the Berlin Natural History Museum, where he found her photograph in the staff list of the website. Although it meant breaking his parole, he booked a plane ticket to Berlin. There was nothing for him in England anyway.

Now Daniel waited for her to wind up the museum stairs towards him, away from the jazz and chatter. He felt perfectly in control of his emotions. He'd waited a long time for this moment. A stuffed flamingo watched from behind glass panels in a pair of doors at his shoulders, along with what appeared to be a badger and a distraught fox with a bulging neck and moulting fur. Daniel did not believe that mistakes happened in isolation; he believed that they cultivated and thickened inside us over a lifetime, waiting to occur. He couldn't blame circumstance or luck for the transgressions of his own life any more than he could let Cathy blame circumstance for hers. Turning points were not bound to fate but to each person's deeply rooted, inescapable nature. He touched the wall to stabilise himself as she moved nearer to him.

Cathy tried her best to smile. She felt a little giddy from drinking that glass of champagne too quickly and wished she hadn't. The darkness on the landing had a formal quality, like a theatre before the curtains came up, and her heart was beating fast inside her rib cage again. Cathy held her fox mask in one hand and her toy soldier in the other. Daniel nudged his lion mask off his eyes onto his head so it pushed his curly hair off his face like a painoly of a fascinator. His grey eyes were duller than she remembered, and sunken in shadowy grey skin scratched with crow's feet. He looked much older than he ought to have done. Standing there in front of him felt unearthly. It was the convergence of decades and his body appeared enormous, as if it were filling the entire staircase and corridor just with his shoulders.

"Do you remember Louis XVII's rhino in Paris?" he said now, instead of hello. That's not what she would have expected him to start with.

"Yes, I remember him," she said carefully. "You claimed he looked like a cross between a war tank and unicorn."

It was a stuffed rhino they'd visited once, murdered by revolutionaries during the French Revolution and displayed at the Paris Natural History Museum. For her twenty-first birthday he'd taken her to Paris and bought her too many presents. It was two years into their relationship. He was making money from the haulage company then and he'd wanted her to feel pampered, but she'd acted like they were still in Essex and eaten with her fingers in posh restaurants then licked them clean, which she knew he hated. She'd put her baseball cap on the table, itched under her armpits on the metro. Out of all the intricate knickers and dresses he bought her that weekend the only gifts that really made her smile were objects she'd chosen herself from a natural history dealership called Deyrolles on the left bank of the river Seine. She chose a pinned blue butterfly in a glass-fronted shadow box along with a shiny green seashell that fitted exactly in her fist. At midnight on her twenty-first birthday she'd sat curled on the hotel sofa still wearing the grubby tracksuit and baseball cap that he'd been trying to get her out of, surrounded by unopened shopping bags of nicer clothes but happily cradling a luminous green shell in her palm. She'd wiped her nose with the palm of her hand. Across her lap was the pinned navy-blue butterfly. She was usually slow to smile but she'd smiled that night, observing how the spray of paler blue made symmetrical patterns on each wing. It had been a good weekend.

Cathy stood at the top of the staircase and raised her eyes to his.

"I spent years trying to make you wear a dress, and now here you are, all grown up and it had nothing to do with me. You look beautiful, Kit-Kat."

Her mouth went ahead and smiled slightly when he said her old nickname. A tick, a neurological betrayal, not just her brain against her body but one part of her mind vying for autonomy against a simultaneous version of her desires. As she pushed the muscles of her face firmly down again she wondered if he'd noticed the renegade smile. Her body felt strange. She wiped her nose with the back of her hand and stopped herself from finishing that gesture from childhood.

"How are you?" he said.

"Fine," she said. "I'm okay."

They paused.

"Aren't you going to ask how I am?"

"How are you?" She hoped her face was expressionless.

"Depends. Did you like the amber beetle this morning?"

"What girl doesn't like being given an entombed, blood-sucking carrier of tropical disease on a Friday morning?" She tried to be glib. "Why are you here?"

"I hoped you might spare me a minute of your evening?" He put his hand on her shoulder and she was rooted to the spot. Daniel's hands were heavy driftwood objects, not the hollow webbed kind of flotsam or jetsam that bobbed on the sea but the gnarly kind that was cumbersome to drag home through the sand.

He didn't continue. He was carved into a complicated

shape, a piece of history, and when his skin was on her shoulder in the darkness she felt the record of all their labyrinthine touches. People needed to be touched to be truly understood, just like objects. A polar bear claw or a toucan beak holds traces of the animal's life boiled down into keratin and dust. You could get a glimpse of a seashell's history only if you ran your thumb along every strange angle and opening on its body. You couldn't understand a butterfly or moth until your fingers had spread its wings. He squeezed her shoulder.

A Toy Soldier

S HE'D WANTED TO know how everything worked, as a
child: how a bird's wing fanned out like it did and how big
a fox heart might be; why eyeballs didn't fall out of eye sockets
and what butterfly wings were made out of. She found a dead
jackdaw frozen in the mud the day she first met Daniel and
his younger brother Jack. It was lying amongst frosty seaweed
and slimy rope under the mouldy cladding of the chalet next
to Cathy's where the air smelt of methane and rot.

She'd scooped the body up and laid it down in the light to
study the frozen blood tangled in its whiskers. It was frigid
and his head was tilted proudly upwards. She opened its beak
to see a flat black tongue, wondering how it connected to
the throat. She stretched the wings and let them fan back. A
three-inch bloodless wound was hidden under the right wing
and she pinched the edge, a white resin fanning out from
muscle underneath. She picked up a stick to break the curtains
of gluey stuff, pulling the skin back even further over the
muscle-covered sternum until she could see it all, the colour
of dried red wine and slimy to the touch. The skin had peeled
right off like a glove.

She was concentrating so deeply that she didn't notice a
boy of her own age step out of the derelict house next door
and stand on the deck frowning at her. The boy had black
curly hair and a beak-like nose. He was as pale as she was. It

crossed her mind that he was a ghost, only he wore frail silver glasses. Ghosts don't wear glasses.

The other houses on Cathy's street had been empty since last summer. People didn't just wander into Lee-Over-Sands, particularly in winter. Its sewage plant and marsh held few attractions. A group of gypsies had settled on farmland behind the sea wall a while back and older boys occasionally came down to smoke and drink in the derelict houses. Those traveller kids smelt of sweat and wood burning stoves and they had cocky swaggers. This bespectacled boy didn't look like a gypsy, though: his expression was timid and his clothes were clean. His green hoodie was from GAP.

Hi, Cathy had said to the boy. The wind whipped her hair and when it brushed over her mouth it tasted of salt. When she moved her fingers up to brush her hair out of the way, her fingers smelt of dead bird.

Morning, he replied. *Do you live here?*

She nodded. Nobody had lived in the chalet next door during Cathy's lifetime. The deck was almost kissing the estuary, sinking down as if the whole structure were about to dive right in. The house was clad with rotting white slats and surrounded by broken cinder blocks. Crisp packets and cigarette ends were frozen into the mud. The windows were mostly boarded up.

Do you live here too? she said.

My brother just bought this place, he said proudly. *He's going to fix it. I'm going to come stay whenever I want.* Cathy turned sideways to note the older brother, who was standing at the window. He had broad shoulders and a bruise on his face like he'd been in a fight. He looked like an adult to her but in fact he was nineteen. He too had curly black hair and a big nose, the same grey eyes as his brother, set deep in his face.

Apricot, a stray cat, padded daintily across the deck rail behind the curly-haired boys, dipping its spine through an assault course of rusty patio umbrella bases and rolls of roofing felt. Apricot was always staring at the sky and being taunted by birds. Cathy wiped her nose with the back of her hand and forgot about the frozen jackdaw's amazing tongue because she was so excited to see a human being of her age. She dropped the bird. It seemed like magic that he'd appeared and even more magic that he had piles of pebbles, shark teeth, plastic cars and toy soldiers at his feet in a red Oxo Cube box. He held a bright red toy soldier in his hand.

My name's Cathy, she said and then, as an afterthought, held out a mouse skull she'd found on the marsh that morning. *And this is my best mouse skull.*

The delicacy of the skull reminded her of the dumb spiders who made webs in the thistle under the decks – castles, almost, with turrets and ballrooms. The spider webs washed away every day while the spiders survived by pulling themselves up to safety on the decking's wood, but a mouse skull was stronger than a spider web.

Cool, Jack had said. *My name's Jack and this is my best toy soldier.* He held the red toy soldier out in his hand for her to look at and got down on his knees so they could see each other's objects better, but once he was down there he wrinkled his nose and said to Cathy: *Your breath's rank.*

Cathy stepped back, hurt, feeling her hopes crumble. Instead of covering her mouth she pursed her lips together and lifted her chin, then spat a gob of saliva the size of a penny right into Jack's face.

Now you smell rank! She'd said, taking a step back and grinning.

Jack took his glasses off to carefully wipe the spit off them. He didn't reply. Jack's brother came out of the chalet doors and Cathy took off, running full speed down the marsh. She kept the mouse skull in her hand but wanted to get as far away from her humiliation as she could.

Get the fuck back here! The brother shouted after her. Cathy's spindly body disappeared off into the bird sanctuary. *Apologise!* Daniel shouted, but she didn't look back. Cathy was not a careful child, not until later.

Tom smoked another cigarette as the police left the scene and curious guests, who'd popped their heads out of the party to watch the police action, filtered away with a good story to tell over more champagne.

Tom headed towards the car park around the side to watch a petite blonde teenager wiping sticky black muck off her body in the dark. She was only wearing a bikini and was shivering, maybe because she was cold, maybe because she was shocked. She was about five foot two and curvy, trying to wipe molasses off her thighs and tummy in the shadows. As he stepped forward the girl stepped back towards the far wall as if she thought he might attack her. They stood a few metres away from each other in the badly lit, empty car park.

"I come in peace," he held up his hands, a cigarette between his fingers.

"It's just treacle," the girl said. "It won't cause any damage, we're strictly anti-violence." She had earnest eyes that made Tom laugh.

"My grandmother lives in Canada on the same street as a molasses factory where a tank once collapsed and a wave 25 feet high killed 21 people and injured 150 people," Tom said.

"You made that up," The protester frowned. Tom adjusted his glasses and inhaled his cigarette.

"It's true. She insists her neighbourhood still stinks of molasses in the summer. Do you want to use my phone to call someone?"

"Thanks. This is really embarrassing. The police took my bag and I'm kind of stuck, you know. Without clothes."

"Sure. It's obviously a problem." He held out his cell phone and the protester stepped towards him. She took the phone and turned away to dial a number, leaving sticky black footprints on the tarmac. Tom reluctantly realised he was going to have to give the girl his suit jacket. She was doing this weird movement with her hands, trying to swat insects off her arms and ants off her feet in the dark while she whispered into his phone. It sounded as if she was leaving an answering machine message. Tom stamped on his cigarette then took his cigarette packet, phone and keys out of his jacket pocket and arranged them in his trouser pockets. He wondered where Cathy was.

"My boyfriend will be here in fifteen minutes," she said with a quick smile as she walked back towards Tom, handing him the phone and brushing hair off her face, streaking it with the sticky black molasses. He held out his jacket for her.

"It doesn't really fit me anyway," he said.

"I can't take your jacket," she said.

"But my arms are too long for it. Honestly. I have

73

ridiculous limbs." She didn't put out her hands to take it, keeping them firmly by her side. He held out his arms to show her.

"I'm so sticky, though," she said. "Your suit will be so sticky after."

"Just leave it by the tree when your boyfriend comes," Tom shrugged. "It's not a big deal. I need a new one." She hesitantly reached for the jacket.

⚜

Down the stairs there was a scrape followed by footsteps and Cathy froze on the landing. She thought it would be Tom coming up from the party to look for her.

"Who's up there?" came a voice from below. It was only Jonas. She leant over the banister while Daniel slunk back into the dark, out of sight. Cathy paused, considered her options, and then called back:

"It's just me, Cathy. I forgot something. I'll be back in ten minutes."

"Sure," said Jonas without coming up any further. "Come down soon, though. Aren't you getting a prize tonight?"

"Thanks Jonas, yes," she said down the stairs and then turned to Daniel as Jonas's footsteps disappeared. The tinny lilt of jazz music drifted up the stairs along with the click of stilettos on wood and glasses clinking.

"You're getting a prize?" Daniel said.

"Yeah."

"Congratulations." He paused. "I went back to Lee-Over-Sands last week," Daniel said. "Your old chalet has been torn down completely."

74

He still hadn't mentioned what she'd done to him. Maybe he didn't know it was she who called the police.

"Are they building something in its place?" It was eerie to think of her little chalet finally expiring, its dirty cladded walls peeling off each other at last, the rotting window ledges cracking, the flat roof wriggling away from the thousands of staples and nails her father and Daniel had forced down into it each winter. The sodden wooden deck, the cinder block stilts, the ugly furniture that had come with the place and had never been replaced. The chalet had been constantly on the brink of collapse throughout her childhood, yet she couldn't imagine it not existing.

"They've been building this two floor, glass-ceilinged monster beach house for a year now. If I'd kept the chalets I'd have finally made some money from it, with people like that turning up. They're using bits of your old house for firewood."

"Firewood?"

"Burning your bedroom walls. Mr Gregg - he's still there on the other side of the sea wall although his wife died - he told me they've not done the foundations right and it keeps flooding."

"Probably not the sort of swimming pool they're used to."

"More a swamp," Daniel smiled. "Mr Gregg still has the swans' nest in his garden."

'How did Mrs Gregg die?" Cathy said.

"Cancer," he said. "Last year."

"She always gave me Hob Nobs."

Cathy and Daniel fell silent, watched by the emus and swans behind the glass door. The swans on Lee-Over-Sands would bite everyone but Mr Greg.

"I missed the North Sea these last years. I missed the

sounds," said Daniel. One of the things she had loved about Lee-Over-Sands was how it was a new world every morning, strangest down on the beach where bars of pebbles reached towards the horizon, constantly making fresh patterns. You blinked and everything changed.

"I think it's a relief not to be near the sea," she said.

Cathy wondered if he still had arthritis in his fingers. Maybe Daniel's hands ached right now, from years of boxing and manual labour. He used to have eczema, too. She used to make Daniel wear oven gloves to bed when they were together, otherwise he'd scratch his skin at night until it bled. It was funny and dismal to remember him like that, a great big man waking up in the morning wearing her mother's pink floral oven gloves. Cathy adjusted the toy soldier in her fist.

He paused, watched her in the dark office, and said:

"What do you have in your hand?"

"Nothing," Cathy replied. She'd always slightly feared he could read her mind, or see inside her. She had obviously been fidgeting with the soldier without realising it.

"Show it to me, I can see there's something there."

She did what she was told, without exactly meaning to, an instinct from the past. The landing felt odd and intimate and she wished it were still yesterday. She opened her fist and took out the toy soldier. If he saw the snake ring with its big ruby eye winding around her finger he didn't mention it. They both stared at the soldier's sloped red shoulders and worn jacket, the shiny black shoes and scuffed face.

"That's Jack's."

Jack died before his tenth birthday, the summer he and Cathy met. Daniel never used to mention his brother, except as a weapon. He used the word to make her shrink and make her stay. He used the word to be forgiven for almost anything he did, to make her feel guilty, and so that word from his mouth still made her flinch. That name connected them with an invisible thread. She knew that if she reached forward and touched Daniel's chest she would feel his heart beating hard, but she didn't do it. She swallowed saliva.

"Your hands are shaking," Daniel said.

"Are you surprised?" she said. "You don't look calm either."

"Did you keep all the objects I sent you?"

Cathy hesitated. "Yes."

"May I see them?" he said.

The two-inch toy was making both their nostrils flare, as if they could smell seawater. He didn't reach out to touch the soldier. The smart little man with his rusty patches and stiff posture hauled Cathy and Daniel back to the marshes.

When Daniel got into bed the last night they spent together in Essex, Cathy had been fast asleep with her face in a pillow and breathing deeply. He hadn't guessed. He'd been working late and was exhausted, so didn't even remember falling unconscious next to her. When he woke up her pillow had a smudge of mascara in the shape of a bird silhouette on it and the sheets were still tangled to her body shape. He said her name, figured she'd be boiling the kettle in their pokey little kitchen, but she didn't reply. He saw that a green seashell was missing from the window ledge and a first shiver of unease passed through him It was usually under the stuffed canary with the big eyes, which he'd bought her the year before from a junk shop in Brighton. She was particular about where she kept her objects.

She used to walk around with the green shell cupped in her hand sometimes, because she said its shape was comforting. Perhaps she was somewhere in the chalet or the marsh with the shell in her hand. Her father had died three months before and she'd been jumpier since, spending longer in the library even after she'd finished her exams, her eyes following him around the room if he was there. He'd had to work harder to make her smile and keep her still. Daniel lay in bed hearing the wheeling and hysterical giggles of seagulls that morning, and felt a white heat rising in his mind. People say losing your temper is 'seeing red' but Daniel always used to see white when it happened, a disorientating white that his mind would be cast far adrift in. It happened more often than he would like, particularly when Cathy was nearby. Before he even noticed that her passport was gone from her underwear drawer and before he tore up their bedroom, his skin had crawled and white light filled his head. He ripped the chalet apart. He shattered the windows and the glass muddled with dried Sea Roses and Yellow Horned Poppies that she'd kept in little bottles on the windowsills. He smashed her Polaroid Camera. He broke the dining room table that he'd made for her and then used pieces of that to break the light bulbs.

When he was done he couldn't breathe, but the white heat in his head was dissipating. Already he missed the colour of her thighs and the smell of her neck. He was out of breath and his hands were shaking. He called taxi firms that might have picked her up. The taxi drivers knew not to lie to him. Nobody had come down to Lee-Over-Sands, but someone had been picked up from town at 3 am that morning and driven to Gatwick. He'd called Essex University and they eventually told him that a last minute work placement had been offered at the Los Angeles Natural History Museum, which was where she'd be spending the year. He'd checked the times of flights to Los Angeles, but it was nearly 10 am by the time he'd worked out where she was going and if she'd been picked up at three, she'd be long gone. The university registrar wouldn't say where she would be staying in California, or how long she'd known that she would be going, but he'd find out easily enough. Marcus had friends all over the world. There must have been visas, credit cards, details, all of which she'd organised behind his back while pretending everything was fine. He lit the barbecue and filled it with bits of his dining room table, watching Cathy's Polaroid photographs and handwriting burn down to ash. Daniel enjoyed watching Cathy's things disintegrate that morning she left him. The blaze smelt revolting, mixing with a gust of wind that had blown over the sewage plant. Yet the strange thing was that after she had been gone a few hours and her things were burning, he'd felt oddly elated. He'd looked out on the sea and for a moment felt an extraordinary sense of potential. He'd been untethered. The morning she left him he slowly, watchfully, set everything alight in the bonfire. He had no idea that the following afternoon the police would come to search the chalet. He hadn't for a second thought she would do that to him, yet they knew exactly where to look and this could only have been because of Cathy.

A Heart Tattoo

CATHY LED DANIEL up one more flight of stairs and through a network of galleries towards her office, where she kept her private memory museum. Most of the doors had glass panels in them so guests could marvel at a library containing a baby gorilla skeleton or a bone storeroom packed with toothy wolves marching away on bare wood floors. In one huge room, thousands of winged creatures were all poised in the darkness as if waiting for something to happen and a few skylights spread city light into the room. Daniel followed her obediently past hundreds of grinning marionette skeletons: kingfishers, parrots, swans. The parrots retained a particular air of sweetness, tilted eagerly forward with beaky smiles. Their wing bones stuck out at the joints as if hoping to begin a conversation or set off from their labelled blocks.

Outside the windows the sky was luminous blue, without a single cloud or breeze. Berlin's clubbers would only just be waking up now, nocturnal, yawning to stretch danced-out limbs and getting ready to become lost again in the city's abandoned factories and power plants. While the museum was frozen in time the acid-addled punks would have stopped drawing trippy chalk sketches on the pavement outside her and Tom's flat and would be drinking cans of beer in doorways. Families would be walking home from dinner and pushing their buggies over glinting *stolpersteine*, stumbling stones, brass plates embedded in the streets engraved with the names of Holocaust victims. Ghosts winked under your feet. Little traumas and memories in the shape of abandoned buildings that reminded you this was a city full of erasures. The city had a strong aversion to forgetfulness. It trapped the past and held onto the ruins, two-faced, one set of features looking forward and the other squinting backwards. It attracted wanderers but kept its history close. Cathy felt both entirely alien and perfectly at home here in Berlin.

"You remember the museum in Brighton, Kit-Kat?" Daniel said. She and Daniel would visit natural history museums together, at first, when the relationship was at its calmest. Falling in love with Daniel when she was nineteen was an experience as intimately connected to whale ribs and lion teeth as it was to the tides on the Essex marshes. They used to spend their weekends at the London Natural History Museum staring at giant hummingbird cabinets and intricately labelled moth collections, even though he didn't care about museums. He did it for her.

"Of course," said Cathy.

Cathy and Daniel also used to visit the Grant Museum of Zoology in central London, lingering in that tiny single-room place cluttered floor to ceiling with shelves of toucan skulls and baby mole bodies preserved in jars. They used to spend weekends in Brighton, visiting moths in the Booth Museum and dusty ornaments in backstreet bric-a-brac shops. When Daniel started making more money they went to the Venice Natural History Museum and the Paris Natural History Museum and held hands under café tables. She couldn't remember much of what they spoke about or ate or did the weekend they went to Paris for her birthday, when they'd seen the stuffed rhino that had once belonged to Louis XVII. One sunny moment of intense awe was embedded in her mind. They'd been in the Gallery of Comparative Anatomy. Sunlight had poured down from vast windows over thousands of bones, cloaking each creature in sunshine. Her recollections of that day weren't visual, more a feeling of Daniel on the other side of the sunlit bone room. She'd felt gutted by loving him in that moment, her fingers tingled with it and her stomach churned.

"I like the giant polar bear in the main gallery downstairs," he said. Cathy kept walking through the museum into a room of bird skins with labels tied to their feet, like human bodies in morgues. They appeared closer to life in this prone posture than they did in the main gallery, where stuffed birds were forced into wily caricatures of their former selves and mounted on platforms.

"He's from Alaska and his name's Qannik," Cathy said. "Inuit for Snowflake. He was shot because he was terrorising a village there."

"A man-eating snowflake."

She slipped Jack's toy soldier from her fist back into her handbag. He watched her do this. By her calculation she still had time before she had to go down and collect her prize. She led him away from the party, and into her office.

Cathy and Jack spent most of that cataclysmic summer playing with half-crushed fox heads, yellowing shards of bone with gnawed edges and toy soldiers on the beach. She liked to catch moths in jam jars, watch them stagger and flutter and then release them back onto gusts of air. She didn't pin moths then. She liked to observe the marsh through her father's salt-blurred binoculars: caramel-coloured dandelions growing out of the mud under her feet, a vast white sky, her mother's underwear hanging off the laundry lines amongst broken garden furniture. That underwear was always soaring off into the Essex marsh and being picked up by birders like her father, who'd said: she's going to kill a finch with those pants one day.

Did you know that sharks have no bones? Did you know that it would take less than six months to get to the moon by car at 60 MPH? Jack used to tell her all about cars and sharks the summer they met, but he didn't know the names of birds or how tides worked or even where babies came from. He was wide-eyed and innocent, somehow, despite having a brother like Daniel with his leggy girlfriends and beer cans and roll-up cigarettes. Once she told Jack that a smooth sea-glass fragment was a precious diamond, created when sea boils at a constant temperature for over a hundred years and turns sea foam bubbles into rock. She traded her bit of common sea-glass, of which she had over a hundred pieces, for one of his biggest shark teeth and he thought this was a good deal until Daniel told him otherwise. Cathy and Jack became a two-person investigation team that summer, scrutinising everything from beetle wings to tidal patterns. They became allies against the tides, partners in beach-combing, shell-collecting, late night ghost stories and moth watching. It was always Cathy who led the charge and Jack who followed, adjusting his glasses and tripping over his feet.

In Essex Cathy used to show off to Jack with all she knew about bird species and habits, but also told him all about animals that didn't really exist, with names like Mooklocks and Gillygaloos and Banshees. Cathy would make up elaborate stories about foxes that walked on their hind legs, eagles without eyes, butterflies that created storms with their wings. Jack almost always believed her, or pretended to. Jack was so earnest, with his little spectacles and frizzy dark hair, his gap-toothed smile. She told him that dodos became extinct because their flesh tasted of sugar and they all ate each other. A duck's quack doesn't echo, and nobody knew why. Nobody knows.

Daniel had just been a shadow in the background that summer, a semi-adult who got angry when they came back late or messy. He was a voice laughing with some girlfriend in his bedroom, or watching TV on the sofa. He smelt of Lynx and marijuana, at least that's what Cathy's mother once said. Cathy and Jack had liked tormenting Daniel's girlfriends, who all had glossy lips and tight skirts, often with high-heels that got stuck in the mud if they tried to step anywhere away from the chalet. Cathy and Jack put spiders in their make up bags and used their underwear as slingshots. The girls rarely came over more than twice. One time Cathy and Jack looked through the bedroom window and saw Daniel with his back to them on a chair, with a naked girl straddling him. Cathy stuck out her tongue at the girl, who flipped her middle finger up without breaking rhythm. Daniel had shuddered and the girl arched her back, still half looking at the kids staring in through the window.

Daniel was trying to teach Jack to swim that summer, but Jack hated getting his eyes salty. Cathy would sometimes come along to their lessons and slide under water like an eel, showing off, grabbing Daniel's and Jack's ankles. Jack would always stay where his feet could touch the floor. He liked to be in control of himself. The three of them used to make fires on the beach, finding dry driftwood and sticks for kindling, small twigs and grass for tinder. Daniel taught them how to set the tinder alight with matches and blow lightly on the base of the fire until it grew, adding driftwood. He always used to let matches burn right down to his fingers, just to see Cathy and Jack scream. The most exciting moment was when the driftwood debated its ignition, resisting for a moment before allowing itself to shiver and flare. Frayed newspaper would rise up and float, slow motion. Jack would get scared and move away from the fire then, because he was a bit of a scaredy-cat. However much Daniel tried to persuade Jack to ride his bike faster, dive under water, and stand closer to the fire, Jack remained steadily sure of his limits. Cathy would lean forward, fascinated, to watch Daniel burn doll arms until the plastic skin blistered and it lost its shape. She helped him attach melted Barbies to Action Man torsos. They'd let them dry fastened together like Siamese twins. Many of Jack's toy soldiers met similar fates, melted during apocalyptic fires and embedded with bits of Lego from fallen buildings. Daniel's eyes would be bright. Jack would tell him to stop and Cathy would tell him to keep going.

Daniel referred to their precious object collections as *The Museum of Jack* and *The Museum of Cathy*. *Pick up your museum*, he'd say. *Is this part of The Cathy Museum or The Jack Museum?* He'd hold up some stray shell or toy. *If you don't pick up your museum from the floor I'm going to throw it all away.*

There was a fair near the caravans at Seawick and they weren't allowed to go without an adult, but it was worth the risk of being late home, just to escape the spooky quiet of Lee-Over-Sands. One evening at Seawick Cathy found a bunch of fake tattoos on the ground and told Jack that he could put them on her, if he liked.

Cathy and Jack stood round the back of the dodgems

next to a chain link fence that faced towards barley fields; the air smelt of passing sewage, stale cigarettes and popcorn. Sometimes, when the wind changed in Lee-Over-Sands, for a second you could smell sewage in the air from a plant up-wind from the beach. *They didn't put that in the brochure when you spent our savings, darling, did they?* her mother would say. Jack held the butterflies, hearts and skull and cross-bone tattoos in his little hands. Over his shoulder Cathy could see the duck-hook game that was impossible to win, but nobody noticed them back there. Fairground workers laughed and swore within earshot. Colourful lights flicked in the darkness.

You have to take your top off, Jack said. *The butterfly needs to go just above your belly button, I reckon.* She remembered her skin tensing with the salty breeze. He licked the inky picture on waxy transfer paper and got down on his knees in the ground to press it onto her stomach.

He put a heart with an arrow through it on the bony area between where her breasts would one day be. She was not girlish. She was a vehement tomboy, but it crossed her mind that when she was a grown-up she might fall in love with Jack. He was solemn and flushed as he licked each picture and pressed it onto her skin for the required minute then peeled the paper slowly away, leaving a wet picture on her body. That part of her skin would be cold for a moment.

It was no more sexual than being huddled in her bedroom telling stories about the ghost of St Osyth, a seventh-century East Anglian Queen beheaded in the wood behind the village church, or riding their bikes down the big hill near Point Clear and curving at the last minute to stop from flying straight out into the sea. Shadows filtered past from the dodgems.

His cheeks were flushed with colour as he touched her. It

was getting late and they ought to go home or they'd get in trouble. It was all a revelation, an uncurling towards adulthood. She wished she'd reached up on tiptoe and kissed Jack that evening at the fair. She would have done if she'd known what was going to happen to him.

⚘

If the protesters had aimed to disrupt the party with their fake oil spill, they'd done a terrible job. The guests in the three interconnecting galleries were all drinking more than they'd meant to and laughing louder, eating canapés and discussing the police drama. Tom was a little tipsy. The music had gained in tempo and the double bass player kept spinning his instrument on the stage.

"What do you call a fly without wings?" Tom said as he approached a colleague. She smiled condescendingly, waiting for the punch line. "A walk. Cathy loves that joke. Have you seen her? The prizes will start soon."

"Sorry, no," said the colleague. "She's probably having some involved conversation about moth wing patterns in the back, right?"

"If you see her, give me a call?" Tom said.

"Course."

"Why wouldn't they let the butterfly into the dance?" said Tom. "Because it was a mothball." His audiences smiled without laughing. "Obviously," added Tom and walked off.

He hoped she was deeply involved in some geeky minutia of entomology. When Cathy was doing her PhD she used to bring caterpillars home to their apartment when they were in the process of turning into moths. It's hard to really know

87

someone until you live with them. It's all very well going to the cinema and sleeping over twice a week, but you don't know a person until they – for example – fill your bathroom with mutating caterpillars and stay up all night sitting on the bathroom floor under phosphorescent lights to watch them and make notes. Or until you watch them iron their underwear on Sunday. Genuinely, she ironed her knickers. She owned a cupboard full of almost the same white shirts, like a uniform. She cleaned the kitchen until it sparkled every night before bed. She said that where she grew up, you just couldn't get bed linen dry, so mould grew in the creases. She said her hair used to smell of mud and that the bathtub in her house was so rusty that the water was always the colour of diluted blood. So now she liked things to be immaculate. Somehow in Los Angeles, despite every second block of apartments having a swimming pool and the sea being just around the corner, she'd always managed to avoid swimming without it being a big deal. She'd never brought her swimming costume, or she wouldn't feel well. It was only in Berlin that he found out that she was scared of water. She grew up on the coast but hated swimming. Even swimming pools freaked her out and she'd refuse to get in them past where she could stand. Other idiosyncrasies just made him smile. She often laughed to herself, little chuckles and smiles he wasn't sure she was aware of. She also watched cartoons when she was alone. Never with him, but sometimes he saw them on her computer or walked in on her watching *Tom and Jerry* or *Roadrunner*. She brushed her hair exactly a hundred times before she fell asleep. He didn't know how much he could love her until they moved in together in Berlin and explored a new city together, taking photos of each other with fairy-tale sculptures in

Friedrichshain park and lounging on man-made beaches by the river.

In Los Angeles she'd always been a listener rather than a talker. She didn't seem really to trust him until he'd agreed to leave Los Angeles with her. Her frown the day she told him she'd been offered a job in Berlin had broken his heart. She'd said she wanted a clean start and he'd thought she wanted to go alone, but actually she'd wanted a clean start together. It wasn't necessarily the best career move for him, but it wasn't difficult for him to get a job at the same museum and it was worth it to see the smile on her face when he said he'd come with her: she claimed it was the nicest thing anyone had ever done for her. She said it was the happiest day of her life.

During silences that first year together, he would have to fight the urge to launch into an anecdote or tell another bad joke just to fill the quiet. She was reserved and he was used to actresses and extroverts, yet her silences were more interesting to him than the intimate and easy monologues of his previous girlfriends. Cathy would sit so absolutely still, opposite him at dinner or next to him in the car, and the expression on her face always had a sort of magic to it. She wasn't beautiful in the way other girls he'd dated were, but the attraction he felt towards her was more intense. Sometimes it worried him, because he imagined the other people who might have had the same reaction.

Two people, she'd told him early in their relationship. *I lost my virginity to a boy who lived in a caravan near my house when I was fifteen.*

And the other?

I had a boyfriend from age nineteen until I moved to Los Angeles.

Did you go to university with him?

No, he lived in a chalet a few doors down. He drove lorries.

A truck driver? Tom had smiled and then regretted the smile because she quickly looked at the floor and her cheeks flushed. That sort of tone was the reason she didn't like to spend too much time with his parents.

Shall we order Chinese food tonight? She'd changed the subject.

She had never quite been able to relax with his parents. His mother had admitted to Tom that she thought Cathy was tightly coiled. *She has uncanny poise*, his mother had said, not as a compliment. His friends also thought she was too different from the extrovert prom-queen types he'd previously dated. His friends teased him about being so smitten with this aloof, occasionally awkward, quiet English girl with a scar on her forehead and long auburn hair. Everyone was against him following her to Berlin. There was something impermeable about her when they first met her, as if she lived only in the present tense without a past or a future. Tom had fitted together other pieces of her past slowly, as if he was building up the history of an archaeological site.

One of the strangest thing about her that he discovered in Berlin was that it wasn't entirely true that she didn't drink, which is what she'd always maintained. She was normally so self-contained and still, yet after they moved in together she would occasionally disappear for a night without calling or coming home. She'd probably done this in Los Angeles, too, but they weren't so close then. In Berlin it had happened five times that he knew of. Every time he'd gone out to look for her, but usually had no luck. She'd eventually come home of her own accord, reeking and penitent. On the third time he actually found her, at four am, after many hours searching all over Neukölln. She'd managed to get quite far out, to a bar near *Treptower* Park and the derelict East German amusement park that where you could book guided tours during the day and into which teenagers snuck at night to have sex and shoot up. He'd found her in a basement sports bar with a neon cigarette sign outside it and dirty windows. Cigarette smoke hung low in the air and chalky-faced East German men were bent over their beers. It was a pocket of the city where you rarely heard people speaking English. Tom stepped inside, not expecting her to be there, but there she was playing pool with a bunch of drunks. Her hair was scraped back into a high ponytail and her skin had a cellophane sheen to it. She was laughing too loudly. She had none of the stillness or the quiet that he'd come to associate with her and for a moment he genuinely thought maybe it wasn't her, just someone similar. She'd tripped over her feet and he took a step forward to catch her in case she fell. The men all turned towards him. She didn't fall over, but grinned at him.

I've been looking everywhere for you. What are you doing?
Playing pool, she said.

Leave the girl alone, a man holding the snooker cue said. *She's just having fun.*

You need to come home, Tom said to her and then, out of nowhere, she reached over and threw a yellow snooker ball right at him with a look of intense, almost comedic, concentration. He dodged the ball and it hit a table behind him, sending beer glasses smashing to the floor and the barman swore, stepping out from behind the bar.

Fuck, Cathy. Chill out, Tom said. As he stepped towards

Cathy she threw two more snooker balls, one hitting his shoulder pretty hard. It was so unlike her.

Don't tell me to chill out, she slurred as he took her arm and twisted it behind her back enough to keep her still without hurting her. As she struggled he pushed her face down against the snooker table until she stopped wriggling.

Get her out of here, the barman said.

She had one cheek on the green table and drool coming from her mouth. He glanced away from her smile and pulled her up to standing position.

Hit me, she'd said. There was snot in her nose and her breath stank.

We're going home.

Hit me, she said. *Please hit me.*

You're wasted.

Hit me, she said.

Let's go.

He began to walk her out of the bar, leaving fifty Euros for drinks and broken glasses. At the door she waved goodbye to the men around the snooker table and they waved back, a little baffled.

Hit me? she said more quietly to him outside the bar, her body so limp that he had to support almost all her weight. They got into the cab and her head lolled against his, but every so often she'd say *hit me, hit me*.

A few hours later, after she'd spent some time throwing up, she cried in the bath while he sat next to the tub, watching her and making sure she didn't fall asleep. She sometimes didn't seem to know herself at all. He could see that there were fragments of her self and her past that Cathy went to a great deal of trouble to suppress. He knew she'd be embarrassed for weeks after this, although probably wouldn't remember the details of what had happened.

Armadillos always give birth to quadruplets, she said. Tom had one hand in the warm bathwater, swishing bubbles.

If you won't talk to me, maybe you should see someone, a professional.

You're so American, she said. Outside the bathroom window techno music played in a passing car.

Astronauts in the first American space station grew 1.5-2.25 inches as a result of zero gravity, he replied. *Being American isn't so bad.*

The human eye blinks an average of 4,000,000 times a year, she said.

4,200,000, he replied. *I think.*

I once skinned and boned a seagull, she said. *I found it on the marsh and I was bored so I buried it to take all the skin off it and cleaned the bones and used glue and wire to put the skeleton back together again. I gave it to my dad as a Christmas present.*

Tom had smiled and tucked her hair behind her ears, pleased with this revelation.

I did the same thing with a dead cat I found once, he said, which was true. He'd found it in the back yard and his dad had helped him put it back together over the course of his summer holidays. *My dad and I named the skeleton Garfield.*

We do have something in common after all, she'd said and he felt stung by her words, as if she'd just slapped him. He took his hand out of the bath and turned his back on her, but without leaving the bathroom. He watched her sleeping that night. Those last words while she was in the bath haunted him more than all the rest of the evening. He'd thought he'd loved others before her, but when he fell for Cathy it was an entirely different emotion. It was stickier yet also clearer: he could look a hundred years into the future and still see them tangled in bed sheets. He badly wanted to understand her.

A Human Tooth

CATHY PUT HER fox mask and bag down on her neat laminate desk; Daniel left his own mask on his head. The long room had two doors in it: the one they'd just come in through via interlocking storerooms and the bird galleries and another, leading towards the opposite wing of the museum. A Polyphemus moth was pinned on a colleague's desk, its brownish-yellow wings five inches long with a pattern that resembled owls' eyes to confuse predators in the dark: witty evolution! The metallic wings of a Morpho butterfly caught light from the windows and sent it shooting off in different directions. Cathy reached for her little brass cabinet key in the pages of her *Encyclopaedia of Insects*. Her cabinet creaked as the doors opened and Daniel stepped towards her.

She pulled a drawer open and he immediately ran his finger along a fish spine he'd sent her when she'd first left him. The line of vertebrae almost wriggled. She caught her breath as he moved a blue Trapezium Conch shell from its place. He held up her Kissing Beetle, rubbing its amber cage in his fingers.

"It makes me happy you kept everything," he said and gave her a satisfied, irritating, smile, telling her this was just what he'd expected from her.

He touched a dried seahorse and an alligator tooth and frowned at the stuffed white tiger with wonky eyes that he'd won for her at Clacton Pier one summer.

His gaze stopped on a red plastic wristwatch, flat on the

green felt with its hands stuck at eight minutes past twelve. Jack's watch. There were small toys from her childhood, including plastic soldiers that had been melted together into a single mutant warrior, a parking lot of Micro machine cars, and a metal Oxo Cube tin. The tin box still smelt a little of sea air and rotting mud, or she imagined it did, the salt clinging to its grooves. Cathy watched his expression: his skin was glossy and his eyes bloodshot.

"You still have all his things," he said quietly.

She was acutely aware of the silence and stillness around them as he reached for Jack's red Oxo Cube box from one of the drawers. She'd hidden all Jack's stuff when she and Daniel got together, because it upset him. Around six inches long and four inches wide, the box had become oxidised, with a shiny black patina inside. This was the box in which Jack had always kept his most important objects. It felt as if Daniel was reaching his fingers into Cathy's brain and plucking a memory out. The moment was surgical, severing connections and re-mapping patterns. As Daniel's big thumbs touched Jack's tin Cathy could have been sitting on the deck in Lee-Over-Sands next to her best friend, plump and bespectacled and eager, surrounded by their beachcombing finds. She could have been ten years old out in the salty cool morning air, holding pieces of perfectly round sea glass or driftwood carved by the sea into funny shapes as the tides shifted gloomily around them.

Daniel took the objects out of her cabinet and put them on her desk: micro machine cars, matchboxes of soldiers and shark teeth, the watch, a pair of little silver glasses with the words 'Whizz Kid' engraved on the slightly bent left arm. The skin around Daniel's eyes tensed and she saw the pulse in his neck. He knocked the cars with his clumsy arthritic hands so they were no longer in straight lines.

"Yes," she said.

Cathy touched the mouse skull she'd found the first day she met Jack and Daniel, because she did not want Daniel to touch it first. Inside it still had chambers intact where the brain had been once. Daniel picked up one of Jack's many matchboxes and pushed it open with his thumb. Inside were some baby milk teeth and a single adult molar tooth with long clean roots. As he picked up that molar tooth Cathy allowed her tongue to find the gap at the back of her teeth where that molar used to be.

"You knocked that tooth out," said Cathy. She had an unwelcome image of making love to Daniel on her little orange boat and the way he used to rock it to scare her. One time he'd pushed her in to the sea and she'd screamed. She'd climbed out onto the mud bank and they'd fucked there with a full moon making animals howl on the marsh. She'd been so aware of her body, always, when he was nearby.

"It's so messed up that you have all this. They're disaster mementos. You're like one of those freaks who collects poker chips from the Titanic and souvenir debris from earthquakes."

Unexpectedly, Daniel laughed and showed his own teeth.

"So you're comparing our relationship to the *Titanic?*"

"There are similarities, no? You were leading lady and iceberg I think."

"I'd say we were more of an earthquake."

"Was I not romantic enough?"

"Depends if you define romance as sending a girl souvenir bird skulls and animal teeth from prison for two years."

97

"Those were reminders, not souvenirs."

"You shouldn't be here," she said.

He reached over then and took her jaw in his hand. She let him. She couldn't look him in the eye as he opened her mouth and put his thumb inside. As if she was a horse he ran his thumb along her lower back teeth until he found the gap he'd once created. He put the tip of his thumb right in its raw cavity and it made her shiver. All her fractures and scars throbbed at the same time, as if worms were wriggling out of each spot of remembered pain: her right knee, scars on her stomach, her fractured finger bones. She felt a familiar and wrong sense of longing.

"I've just missed you," he said, his fingers still inside her mouth. She didn't say anything, her throat constricted by his taste, and her emotion. "I know I messed up and hurt you badly, and I deserved what you did to me. I've learnt my lesson."

When he released her she felt dizzy with the lingering taste of him in her throat. Her chin was warm where it had rested on his hands. The papier mâché mask still sat on top of his head. His doughy face was marked with sunspots, his nose and cheeks uneven. Cathy could see, somewhere in the furrowed skin around Daniel's brown eyes, the nineteen-year-old boy who'd moved into the chalet next to hers when she was ten and loved building fires out of driftwood on the beach.

"Do you remember the canary I bought you in Essex?" Daniel said in the gloom of the museum. They could only just hear the party below, the noise floating up through libraries and the store cupboards underneath Cathy's office. It was a long room cut into cubicles by an assault course of shelves, old cabinets and cork boards covered in drawings. There was an elephant skull watching them, and an owl.

"Sure. He was beautiful," Cathy said.

"You left him in Essex."

Daniel was happy she'd kept all his gifts, objects which hadn't been easy to send from prison. His friends on the outside had thought he was crazy, making them send feathers and shells and skulls to some girl in Los Angeles. Marcus helped at first because Daniel hadn't let anyone else's name slip, but two years into Daniel's sentence there was a raid on the garage and thirteen drums of lubricant were found stashed with heroin and amphetamines. Marcus was jailed for sixteen years and Riley, Daniel's replacement, for twelve. So in a way Cathy had helped Daniel.

"What happened to the other things I left in the chalet?"

"I burnt most of them before the police came," he said and she raised her blue eyes to him, obviously unsure if he was serious or not. "They thought I was burning evidence, but I had no idea what was about to happen." He paused. "Do you ever get the urge to re-arrange the stuffed animals in the dioramas in the museum at night? Or the birds in that giant gallery?"

"No."

"Do you ever think how you'd like to be taxidermied?"

"No."

"I'd have us dancing."

"We've never danced. Not once. I think we'd be some grotesque diorama, a beast with two backs."

"What does that mean? A beast with two backs?" he said.

"It's a Shakespeare quote. *Othello*."

"Show off." He smiled. "Have you missed me?"

"I haven't missed you," she said. "Not for a moment."

"Liar," said Daniel.

The first time Daniel hit her they'd been out on the deck cooking sausages on the barbecue. She was nineteen. He was twenty-eight. He'd been back in Lee-Over-Sands for three months then. His colleagues had been in the chalet all day and a faint smell of cheap aftershave and sweat hung in the air. The clouds in the sky were bunching up as if waiting to rain and a low mist hung over the marsh and the sea.

Does mist like this give you the shivers? Cathy had said. Sausage fat hissed and the waves broke against sand beyond the estuary underneath the deck. Moths hovered at the sliding doors, banging against the glass trying to get to the light. Smoke rose off the barbecue, a slightly different colour from the mist.

Why? He said. She looked at his grey eyes and black curly hair, his big nose and wide shoulders, trying to gauge if he really didn't know what she meant.

Because of Jack?

Clearly he did know what she meant, because the next thing she knew he'd knocked her sideways with the back of his hand. Her head hit the floor a little way from the barbecue. She heard seagulls and waves and then fell unconscious. When she woke up she had a jumper under her head. The fire was out and the food was gone and Cathy walked to her dad's chalet three doors down instead of going inside to see Daniel again. That day she learnt that only Daniel was allowed to mention Jack, and even he would never mention the night Jack died. When she stumbled home her dad was asleep on the mangled sofa in front of a cookery channel, a beer can and a whiskey bottle on the floor in front of him. Cathy washed her face in the sink and the water turned red from where her head had hit the floor and bled. She peed in the toilet, noticing that her dad had stubbed out a bunch of cigarettes even though he knew they blocked the sewage system. She would pick them out in the morning. She couldn't leave Essex. She couldn't leave her dad, or her objects.

You okay, Dad? she said when he stirred.

Tip-top, her dad had mumbled, and then fell back to sleep.

Tom sipped champagne in the museum's atrium and stood in front of a large cedar wood cabinet and a 407.48 carat yellow diamond. The museum director, a distinguished man with an equally remarkable handlebar moustache, was conferring amongst the party organisers, presumably discussing the details of the speech he was going to make. He could see Cathy's boss, a woman with an unflattering bob of black hair and vermilion reading glasses that matched her lipstick. A diamond called The Incomparable announced itself as the third-largest diamond ever cut. He scanned the crowd of guests more intently for her auburn hair and green dress. He pushed his way over towards the solar system exhibition to ask the guard if he'd seen Cathy. Tom was proud of the solar system and the sun, knotted his mouth and narrowed his eyes. The museum had appalling security systems; both the guards and the technology were ancient.

"She'll be down in a minute," said Jonas. "She forgot something."

"I'll just go check on her," Tom said and didn't wait for Jonas to shrug before beginning to lope up the spiral stairs two steps at a time.

The previous night they'd cooked pasta together in their little kitchen with the windows wide to catch the breeze. They'd eaten on their tiny balcony outside the bedroom, amongst muddy plant pots and ashtrays. A mariachi band had passed by under the balcony as they spoke, a group of teenagers had smoked weed in a children's playground, the sun had gone down and when he kissed Cathy she'd tasted of tomato sauce. A cat named Maud, belonging to their neighbour across the hall, jumped onto their balcony and pawed Cathy's thigh while Tom was kissing her.

Evening Maud, she'd stroked the cat. Berlin summer light was beautiful, filling the wide streets and illuminating the pastel building façades.

We should get a cat one day, Tom said.

Cathy loved their flat. She'd never really settled anywhere in Los Angeles, she was always finding reasons to move – broken air conditioning, mad housemates, annoying locations – but the Berlin apartment was her home. She adored the high windows, the white floors and Maud, whom she looked after when the owner went away. The room was opposite *Hasenheide* Park and not far from *Tempelhof*, an abandoned airport turned playground, full of allotments and picnickers. She liked all the open spaces and being able to spend time outdoors. Berlin apartment blocks are often built around courtyards, so what appears from the street to be a single building is in fact a network of apartments. Cathy wasn't particularly sociable, in general, but she had made friends with many of the residents in her building and loved spending time on the picnic benches around the courtyard. Maud's owner was an old man with missing teeth for whom Cathy went supermarket shopping every Saturday. In the flat below was a mother of five children who dyed her hair a different colour every month and invited Cathy in for Turkish coffee. Cathy's closest friend in Berlin was an artist named Jennifer who lived on the ground floor and had recently painted a mural of a safari over the entire front of the building, much to the owner's anger and everyone else's amusement. Jennifer went out clubbing most weekends and would roll home in her leather pants just as Cathy was waking up on Sundays. Leaving Tom to sleep in, Cathy would often go downstairs into the courtyard and watch Jennifer chain smoke cigarettes and mumble about her exploits the previous night. Tom had opened the kitchen window the previous weekend and heard their conversation among the picnic benches while he drank coffee upstairs.

Would you rather try to survive a zombie outbreak or a robot uprising? Jessica had said vaguely, smoking her cigarette.

Zombie. I'm bad with computers.

Would you kill your parents if they became zombies or leave them to infect other people?

Humane annihilation, absolutely.

I bet you wouldn't really, said Jennifer. *You'd create a sleep rota or something and try to invent a cure, valiantly, against the odds.*

No one has the luxury of personal moral codes during an apocalypse. It's survival. And anyway I don't like my mother.

Oh my god, would you be the savage maniac living in the U-bahn tunnels and becoming one with the night?

I'd have Tom in the U-bahn tunnels with me, though. I'd stay with Tom even if zombies bit him.

Apocalypse love, Jennifer had said. *Gross.*

Tom, sipping coffee upstairs, had smiled.

⁂

Cathy thought it was probably a quarter past eight now, but wasn't sure. People would be beginning to worry if she wasn't downstairs soon, getting ready for the prize-giving at nine o'clock. Tom would certainly be worrying.

"You must have missed me a little," Daniel said.

"No," she said, although this wasn't entirely true. She had missed him a great deal when she first left, despite herself, even though for the year before she ran away she used to lie in bed at night and list disasters she'd very much like to befall him. About a year into their relationship they were just small calamities, such as hoping he would trip on his shoelaces in front of his colleagues and or that waitresses would put milk in his coffee when he asked for it black. He never used to say, "I love you", although she knew he did love her. Once or twice she'd found guns in their chalet, casually left in a drawer or on the night stand. On another occasion the place was searched by police officers, but they didn't find anything, because he'd hidden his contraband out on the bird sanctuary underneath an upturned boat. Twice she gave him an alibi, said he was at home when he'd been out late. When he took her to class in the morning she'd stare out of the window and wish him paper cuts between his fingers, the jarring noise of

104

road works when he was trying to concentrate, fifty pound notes left in his jean pockets when he put them in the wash, and empty ice trays in the fridge when he wanted whisky. She wished him lice on his pillows and mould on his new loaf of bread and always being in the wrong queue at the airport. As time went on her imagined disasters became more elaborate. She wished him smashed glass under his feet, unexpectedly sharp knives, drunk drivers, and heart disease. Fatal late-onset allergies to bee stings or peanuts, undiagnosed until it was too late. A pocketknife slipping through his fingers onto bare feet, broken exit signs during fires, traffic accidents, police sirens. She'd sit there and list misfortunes in her head, but when he hit her and left her out on the beach all night, when she woke up in the morning with the taste of blood on her tongue, still she returned to his bed the next night. When he broke her collarbone and she spent a week in hospital, she didn't tell the nurses how it had happened. She could never predict when he was going to hurt her; his was a secret rhythm of anger and penitence.

"Essex was different without you when I went back. It even smelt different, like maybe they'd sorted out the sewage plant a bit. I missed you," he said.

"Will you live there again?" she said politely, although her skin was too hot and her mind was racing. At night she used to dream about how the space between the tendons of his neck would feel under the flat pad of her thumbs, finding their way down to his larynx and then pushing in on it. In her dreams she was so strong that her weight sank him. She'd feel the upward force of his wrists in the grooves of her shoulder as she slept, but she dreamed she was superhuman: the puzzle pieces of their bodies, thumbs and necks, palms and shoulder bones, all forced together with perfect symmetry. She'd wake before the end, shining with sweat and shaking from the exertion.

"Only if you came with me," he replied. Cathy could smell Daniel's body in the warm museum air as they stood close to each other. It was sweat, deodorant, and the tang of swimming pool chlorine. He used to swim every day in Essex, his big body sliding through the surf and then emerging, his curly hair wet, snot in his nose. Each day we breathe about 23,040 times. We can close our eyes and our ears but smell is inescapable. It goes straight from the nose to the hippocampus, the part of the brain responsible for long-term memory. Cathy hated the smell of roses and violets, tweed and old books. Her father had been gin and dandruff shampoo and, later, when he was really ill, rot. Her mother was icing sugar and sleep sweat.

"You could be a carpenter again. You were a good carpenter."

"Will you come home with me, Kit-Kat?" he said.

"No," she shook her head.

"This won't ever be your home," he said. "I'm your home. I'm back."

"You're not my home any more."

Daniel stared at her then – unexpectedly – he looked away, as if he was backing down. He never used to back down.

"What's that one?" Daniel said abruptly, changing the subject, pointing to a tray of green moths on someone's desk.

"African Moon moths," she said.

"This one?"

"Fireflies." Trays of grub-like creatures were attached to minute handwritten labels, each with antennae as long as their wings.

"Didn't you and Jack used to try and catch them in Essex?"

"Yeah." They would flash on July evenings in Lee-Over-Sands and she'd catch them in jam jars. The females were grub-like and flightless with thoraxes that glowed yellow and green. They'd band together on stones and hedges, raising their luminescent abdomens to the moon, waving them seductively from side to side. The winged males fluttered around in high excitement, a bit like moths, but glowing weakly. Their adult lives lasted just a few days, maybe a week at the most and in that time they had to find a mate and have their babies and then expire, exhausted. It was beetle melodrama, frantic passion, courtship dances and competitions for affection, short pleasure and fast death.

Her feelings for Daniel had always been blurred, like a battle going on inside her. For example, when she left Essex for Los Angeles, after months of planning, at the last minute she'd taken one of Daniel's T-shirts with her. She'd been terrified that he'd wake up and stop her but she still doubled back, her suitcase already on the deck, tiptoeing into her bedroom to grab a T-shirt hanging on the edge of the bed where he was sleeping. Perhaps part of her had wanted to be caught or maybe she really did just want to keep his smell, although by the time she arrived in Los Angeles a miniature bottle of her mother's perfume had spilt in the suitcase and the shirt no longer smelt of him. She pretended to herself that she was scared of any reprisal for what she did after leaving Daniel, yet this wasn't the whole story. Far worse than the physical fear was the little masochistic nugget in the back of her mind that told her she was only pretending to be the sort of person Tom could love; that she was in fact still the feral, guilty girl from years ago with bruised ribs and a black eye sitting next to Daniel with her toes in the estuary mud. The level-headed part of her knew she'd probably be dead by now if she'd stayed with him and that she was vastly happier without him. Yet it was this nasty twitch towards the past that truly terrified her, the battle in her mind, the sense that maybe it would be easier to stop pretending and just slink back in time with Daniel. She was scared that it would be easy to go back to the patterns that she knew so well, rather than stay with patterns that made her happy.

She smiled as she stood in her office now. Daniel smiled back, close to Cathy's face. In her lowest moods she wondered if she had called the police not to keep him from coming after her, but as a crutch to stop her from going back to him.

"Let's go downstairs. We can talk downstairs. You're scaring me."

"I'd rather talk here," he said. "You wouldn't be here in this job if it wasn't for me," he said. "You wouldn't have a degree. You'd still be counting moths in Essex. You don't seem very grateful."

Daniel had paid her father's medical bills, and her university fees. She'd known how he got the money, but she took it anyway.

"I'm grateful for everything you did for Dad and me in Essex."

She heard a creak outside her office now. It was probably an old pipe or some other element of the museum building warping in this midsummer heat, beams changing shape or plaster cracking, but she was startled. The building appeared to have been melting this week.

"Cathy?" came the voice of Tom a few corridors over. "You back here?"

Cathy winced. She didn't want Tom to walk in on this.

Daniel obviously didn't, either, because he picked up Jack's objects from the counter. He put some cars, a handful of matchboxes, the watch and glasses in the Oxo Cube box. He picked up her shoes and handbag and came up close to her. She had an urge to touch him and run away simultaneously, so stayed absolutely still and rooted to the spot.

"I want to talk about Jack," Daniel said quietly, under his breath. "I want to talk about the night he died. That's all. Will you do that for me?"

"Yes," she said simply.

There was no other answer she could have given to that question, or nothing her body could have done except lead Daniel quietly through the opposite door from the one she had first brought him through. She took him away from the bird galleries, away from Tom, and into the quiet depth of the museum. During all their time together after it had happened, they'd never actually spoken about the night Jack died. They spoke around it, hinted at it, referenced it but had never had a conversation about it. Perhaps we can never escape our childhoods. We walk around with the ghost of previous selves crouched inside us like mariachi dolls. We can run away, but the past-selves will follow. We can pretend to be rid of these incarnations and tell ourselves we are untethered, but habits and ghosts of the past are always lurking.

Fortune Cookie Messages

TOM IMAGINED CATHY would be bent over her beetle tray, cataloguing something that she'd been meaning to get round to for a while, or practising her speech. When Cathy was in one of her moods she could often be found with her tweezers poised over cigar boxes full of beetles sent in by amateur collectors, envelopes and tin boxes full of uncategorised bugs. The last row of cabinets in the entomology room was devoted to the thousands of miscellaneous creatures the museum received each year: colourful 1920s cigar boxes full of beetles glued to card scrawled over with the smallest of handwriting, whole drawers of matchboxes sent from the Congo or Borneo and others overflowing with mothy envelopes or rolled up scrolls of paper with cotton coming out of either side to hold the uncategorised bugs inside. These disorganised creatures made Cathy nervous. In spare moments she could be found on a ladder there, untangling the wings of ladybugs from the hind legs of Darkling Beetles.

A few months after moving to Berlin they'd had an argument about where they would spend the following Christmas. He'd wanted to meet her mother and hadn't realised that Cathy hadn't seen the woman since she was eleven. They'd been together a little over a year then and he'd known she wasn't close to her mother, but had no idea they were completely estranged. Later he'd found her organising seashells quietly in the museum, referencing them against a giant encyclopaedia. Tom had sat on the floor of with his back against the wall and watched her slim fingers handling shells, her downcast blue eyes flickering a little. Another small instalment of her life came out. She put down the shells and took four little toy ballet dancers out of her pocket. They were boys and girls about two inches high, caught in furious pirouettes with red and blue costumes that had faded over time. Some were missing legs, or arms, but she told him now she'd idolised them all and played games in which they were a circus troupe travelling the world. They were gifts from her mother.

It was unforgivable, Cathy said, that her mother had left her with her alcoholic father in that weird part of the world. Cathy said her mother was dressed in an orange skirt-suit the morning she left, with a little silk scarf around her neck and knee-high black leather boots that squeaked when she walked. She'd smelt of lily-of-the-valley perfume. Cathy had peeked out of the door in her pyjamas and saw suitcases at the door. Her father wasn't around, but he must have known she was leaving because he never once mentioned her absence. They just muddled on.

Cathy had looked so fragile that afternoon after she'd told Tom all this, thumbing the ridges and crevices of her ballet dancers and staring at her hands. Tom had touched a ballet dancer with a blue dress, one step closer to knowing Cathy.

Tom stepped into the solar system exhibition, up past the bespectacled gorilla in the library and the small mammal gallery on the first floor, then up again into the bird galleries on the top floor. He marched through a warren of bird-filled corridors towards Cathy's moth rooms

"Cathy? You back here?" he said as he got near her rooms. The air fell back onto the diluted rhythms of the party down-stairs, which was almost directly underneath.

"Cathy?" he said again.

He loved the museum's empty corridors and laboratories at night, all the cluttered spaces holding their breath ready for the next day.

"Cathy?"

No reply, so he stepped into her office, which was empty. He sat down on Cathy's office chair and flicked on the desk light. A fox mask was on the desk, presumably hers, so she'd been here earlier. He looked at the tray of hawkmoths she'd been busy pinning that week. On graph paper nearby were tidy diagrams of torsos and eyes. He opened one of the notebooks lined up on her shelf and his knee fidgeted as it always did, moving up and down. It knocked against a specimen cabinet under her desk, making one of its doors creak open a half-inch against his knees.

Tom put his hand down onto the cabinet doors. He pushed the chair back and the cabinet door opened a little more. The drawers had typed labels with words like 'phylogeny', 'biogeography' and 'wing polymorphism' on them. He bent down and pulled out one of the drawers open. It was labelled 'mating frequency and *Nosema* prevalence'. Inside, he was surprised to see no boring articles on hawkmoths but odd bits and pieces such as a piece of thin white coral, a tiny magpie skull, and a paper airplane he remembered making from a restaurant menu near their apartment a while back.

He opened another drawer labelled *Hyles lineata* in which there was a doll's head, some bird feather specimens, a pink birthday candle and a cassette tape of *Sleeping Beauty*. The spokes had vomited out a tangle of pink magnetically coated tape and the rivets in the plastic case were covered in what appeared to be mud smudges. He ran his hands over the little pile of her mother's ballet dancers, all still stretching and reaching. Had she given these drawers boring labels so nobody would look in them, or had the labels belonged to the cabinet before she filled it with these curious objects? They were typed so it wasn't obvious.

Tom opened up one of his own sketchbooks, one that he'd thought he'd left on the bus a couple of months ago, which was full of drawings of dinosaurs and parts of Cathy's body. He observed an oak leaf, train tickets, pretty beer bottle tops. He ran his fingers over a single blue leather glove from this past winter – she'd dropped its twin off *Oberbaum* Bridge by mistake. Tom smiled, weighing up how angry Cathy would be that he'd gone through her things with the pleasure of seeing this secret collection.

He'd always been fascinated by how *little* Cathy appeared to own. A few books and pieces of clothing, but her possessions had been minimalist in her various apartments in Los Angeles and now it was the same in their shared apartment in Berlin. He was messy by nature but because it upset Cathy so much when he left dishes in the sink and trousers on the floor, he was now near immaculate. He owned many things himself: engine parts and bits of bone, paintings and movie posters. When they moved to Berlin from Los Angeles she only brought one suitcase with her and shipped just a couple of boxes of what she said was entomology stuff, equipment and books. Obviously it had included the stuff he'd found here.

He felt as if he'd caught Cathy eating toast over the sink. Tom couldn't keep himself from smiling at this cabinet: she was a hoarder. He sat back in her chair. His self-contained girlfriend, who ironed her underwear and rarely wanted to speak about the past, was a secret hoarder of autobiographical objects.

He picked up a bird skull and then a small fish skeleton. He noted the wing bones of a seagull and a couple of fossilised shark teeth. A dried white starfish. Tom unfolded a wad of newspaper clippings in an envelope, opening them under the bright light of Cathy's desk lamp. The first was a clipping with a school picture of a solemn little boy with wiry black hair and pasty skin, a big nose holding up wonky silver glasses. Tom turned away from the newspaper, considering – just for a moment – that this collection was a map that he ought not to read without her permission:

CHILD'S BODY FOUND IN LEE-OVER-SANDS

The name of the child who drowned at Colne Point Beach in Lee-Over-Sands on Tuesday morning has been released. Authorities say nine-year-old Jack Bower of Chelmsford was found on the beach by his brother, Daniel Bower, who had performed CPR. Paramedics were called and pronounced him dead at the scene. Circumstances leading to this tragic death are unclear. Mr Bower, nineteen years old, lived in a chalet on Beach Road and is said to have sometimes looked after his brother during weekends and holidays. Funeral details have not yet been announced.

Tom peeled a photo from the same envelope of the curly haired boy with the silver glasses, this time in a T-shirt and shorts grinning at the camera. He held the hand of a teenager who was presumably his older brother: they looked just like each other. In the background of these two brothers stood an early simulacrum of Cathy, a ragged little girl with bright, bright, bright ginger hair and hundreds of freckles. There was no scar on her forehead. She was wearing an oversized white T-shirt with a diet Pepsi logo on the front.

Tom looked away from young Cathy and folded the pages back up. He touched a pile of fortune-cookie messages, which he guessed were from his and Cathy's favourite Chinese restaurant down the road from her old apartment in Los Angeles. 'A feather in the hand is better than a bird in the air', said one of the fortune cookie messages. 'Actions speak louder than talks'. 'You look pretty'. 'Maybe someday we will live on the moon!'

❧

In the half-darkness Cathy could see soot marks on the walls above the air vents, bits of wall where the plaster was coming off. The windows still let in enough light to see by as they walked through a collection of small mammal skeletons that appeared to march – a ghost army – from wall to wall under a wooden roof. As they stepped deeper into the museum, the music became quieter.

"Let's stop," Cathy said. "Let's talk here. I don't want to go further."

A room to the right was full of gormless plastic Neanderthal mannequins, ranging from bent monkeys to upright humans. The mannequins were all on their sides, arms sticking out of boxes amongst boards with information about evolution. Daniel kept walking. He opened a couple of doors off a skinny corridor, all of which had keys in their doors but weren't locked. One led into an office with a messy desk and walls covered in posters from former exhibitions: 'One Million Years of the Human Story' and 'Whales: Giants of the Deep'. Another was full of filing cabinets and cardboard boxes. Another room had a strange chalky smell coming from the shelves of dried coral against the walls.

"It's quiet in here," he said, and entered.

There was a sink and a small window looking down on a messy courtyard, around which the various wings of the museum were arranged. Daniel washed his face with cold water in the sink. Stone fingers reached out from boxes and jars all over the room with pretty names on their labels: Carnation coral, Tongue coral, Flower Leather coral. Near the sink was a yellow metal cabinet full of bottles with chemical labels. Dusky light came through the one window, outside of which was a bunch of scaffolding. Daniel reached forward and touched Cathy's face, putting a thumb on the corner of her mouth.

"You've smudged your lipstick," he said.

She didn't reply.

"I never thought I'd see you in lipstick. You look pretty."

"I've grown up."

"I can see that."

"I'm getting married."

Daniel kept his eyes steady.

"Congratulations. Is he the geeky American you met in Los Angeles?"

"You had people following me." It was a statement, not a question and Daniel didn't reply. "Why did you stop sending me things? Was it because I left Los Angeles?"

"The lorry company was busted on a big job so Marcus

and that lot became less helpful. If you hadn't called the police on me I would be in jail for a lot longer. I should be thanking you."

"Well don't."

"I'm serious."

"I wanted you out of my life. That's the only reason I did it."

"Consider my gifts as tokens of appreciation, despite your motivation."

He brushed hair off her face and she remained still.

"I understand why you left and I'm still here in front of you saying I love you. Nobody will ever know you like I do."

"I haven't missed you," Cathy said.

"I'm in control now," he said. Cathy raised an eyebrow. "Jack would want us to forgive each other," Daniel said. "And he'd want you to come home."

"You can't use him like that."

"I can say whatever I like about my brother."

The storeroom's air smelt of chalk and Daniel could feel their hearts beating in unison, like he wasn't sure where he began and she ended. He didn't like her tone or the arch of her eyebrows, almost disdainful, or how she appeared to think she had the upper hand over him. He'd imagined this moment so often over the last years, as well as imagining what they would do together after he came to find her. They'll buy a boat, perhaps. They'd ride on the estuary. They'd dance on the deck. She would make objects talk to each other, beer cans to shoes and umbrellas to washing up sponges. They would go back to their origins. In the storeroom of coral he picked up her handbag and took Jack's lead toy soldier out of it, putting it in the palm of his hand. He smiled at her and she smiled tentatively back. He tensed his fists.

I'm a seagull! Jack used to jump on Daniel's bed in the morning, pretending to swoop. Jack often used to pretend he was some sort of bird, racing up and down the beach with his hands outstretched to catch the wind with his anorak flapping behind him like wings. He was a child deeply immersed in his own world, as Cathy was. Watching them play together was almost spiritual, like they might slip out of this life because they were so deep in their heads. Jack could often be found in elaborate battles with ghosts at the end of their parents' garden or in the living room, drop kicking them and punching, but when it came to school friends Jack was the one who was pushed around at bus stops. Daniel always felt fiercely protective of his little brother, with his toothy grin and silver glasses with tape around the nose or safety pins on the arms. He tried to take Jack to the boxing gym with him sometimes, but Jack would forget his trainers or get a stomach ache and end up reading in the dressing room, eating liquorice allsorts. Daniel had wanted to make Jack stronger.

One of the reasons that Daniel persuaded his parents to let Jack come to Lee-Over-Sands so much was that it would be good for him to be outside catching crabs and going on long walks, learning to tie a boat knot and make a fire. But Cathy had succeeded in building Jack's confidence where Daniel had failed. Daniel used to go out to the sea every few days with Jack, hold him afloat while he kicked his legs, but Jack would cry if he got salt in his eyes. Jack was shy with Daniel, as if he wanted to be liked, but Cathy didn't care what anyone thought of her and this rubbed off on Jack. He ran faster in her presence and spoke louder: when she was around, he even tried to go under water sometimes. Daniel's parents saw how Jack came out of his shell after he started spending weekends with Daniel in the chalet.

No credit to me, Daniel had told his father. *It's this ginger kid he fancies.*

Jack started to laugh more once he became friends with Cathy. He no longer clung to Daniel quite so much, he was no longer always standing on the side-lines watching Daniel paint and mend things. Instead he would disappear off into the marsh in the morning and come back in the evening full of stories about birds and burnt-out cars, changing tides and washed-up detritus from cargo boats. His cheeks became pinker and his body less scraggly. Suddenly he had secrets and whispered games.

First thing in the morning you could hear all sorts of strange things on the marshes beyond the street where she grew up. Cathy always liked the moment when the moon was still visible in the sky but the sun was already coming up. It was misty and cool that morning, and it felt as if anything were possible.

A crow, behind Cathy and Jack on the mudflats as they walked from the bridge to the beach, had opened and closed its wings, only just visible in the mire. Jack always climbed out of his bedroom window while she climbed out of hers and they would meet up at the bridge. The early morning air bit their skin and they waded together across a shallow part of the estuary in their Wellington boots. His favourite toy soldier was in his pocket, and her best mouse skull was in her fist. The horizon was invisible and they'd stood up on a mound of grass looking out on the marsh and the murky pebble beach.

The morning she left Jack to drown they'd caught their breath on the quiet ridge and the scream of a gull broke out like a drunk at a party when everyone else was hushed. The rusty remains of a car engine had a small cloud of bees diligently nosing up to marigolds around it. Cathy led Jack by the hand towards the beach where he died, their Wellingtons squelching in the wet sand. In Lee-Over-Sands it was easy to imagine that the water had some sort of consciousness. It was creaturely, the way it crawled and licked.

That's a Banshee, she'd said of a low wailing in the distance. *It's like a fox, but without legs. They push themselves forward with their tail.*

Liar, said Jack, who was becoming less gullible by then, near the end of this cataclysmic summer.

Her past was rising as she stood in front of Daniel in the coral storeroom. Cathy opened the Oxo Cube box and picked out Jack's glasses. They were maybe the most evocative object in her collection of memories, the strangest because they almost used to be a part of his body. Like keeping the bone of a saint. She'd found the glasses amongst hairballs and shadows next to a chocolate wrapper and a broken periwinkle shell under her bunk bed a few weeks after he died. He'd had about five pairs, because he was always losing or breaking them. They all had silver rims and tortoise-shell temple ends that hooked over his ears. They summed him up: owlish, delicate, orderly, wide-eyed, and even though he no longer existed when she found the spectacles under the bed, it was as if Jack was staring at her. This object was his body, a part of Jack's anatomy she'd interacted with all summer. The glasses had watched her do handstands and known to add turrets to her sand castles. She'd folded them and placed them carefully on top of his cars and shark teeth, next to his red watch.

"Underneath that smart dress and lipstick you're still my Cathy," Daniel said.

"I'm not yours," Cathy said, but weakly.

She could sense the familiar places on Daniel's body: how the muscles in his arm used to flex as he kissed her and how his wrist fitted exactly in the curve behind her neck when they were lying down. She did not want these muscle-memories any more than she wanted to remember his smell. Her bare feet wriggled on the scuffed floor. Daniel's breath was hot on the side of her face so her hairs rose up to attention again. He reached over to a desk and picked up a green apple left uneaten by one of her colleagues earlier that afternoon. He took a bite and the juice frothed up. He offered her a bit. She shook her head. The first time he and Cathy fucked was out on her father's deck with water lapping underneath, sunshine hitting her chin and the near-blue of her thighs in a polka dotted bikini. He'd just finished eating an apple and he dropped the core into the estuary before he turned her around to press the axis of her hips into the wooden deck rail in a way that hurt. He bent her over towards the sea like the prow of a boat and when he was finished, a black bug, shiny as the pupil of an eye, had crawled up her Achilles heel over the dune of her ankle while he kissed her, up to the ripples of her knee. Its wings had shrugged slightly, but it kept going, plodding a straight line with almost imperceptible footprints across the top of her thigh onto her hipbone. Daniel had picked it up from her skin between his thumb and forefinger, and then squashed it.

Although she was standing in the museum now, she was on the edge of the world, stomping through marsh water in Lee-Over-Sands. She was on her kitchen floor, her lip bleeding and her legs spread. She was naked on the deck with her spine on mouldy wood. She was waiting to fall unconscious, covering her head with her arms and curled in the foetal position. She was forgiving him as he cried on her lap. It was all happening at the same time in her head. All the breaking and tasting and the mutual, consuming guilt merging with the loneliness that marked both their lives after he came back to Lee-Over-Sands.

Coral

TEENAGE-CATHY WAS YAWNING awake through layers of time as she stood with Daniel in the coral storeroom. Not the fearless child but the teenager who jumped at loud noises and dreamed of pain. She held Jack's Oxo Cube box. Daniel put his hand on her face and brushed a finger down her neck.

"You belong with me," he said.

"I don't belong to anyone," she said.

"You can tell yourself that if you like, but it's not true."

The look in his eyes was exactly the same look she'd known on the Essex marshes. It made her think of blood and she didn't like it. Staring at him now, she saw his face was hard and his lips thin. They were so close they might have kissed. She could smell his breath. If she allowed herself to be weak now her whole life would change. She would go back to the marshes, to the mud and the salt water, to the little barbecue and the smell of damp and every time mist fell on the marsh she would feel sick with guilt about Jack; and Daniel, probably, would start to hurt her again. Her bones would ache when she slept and she'd add new scars to the museum on her skin. She didn't want to fall back in time like that, to an earlier and sadder incarnation of herself. She wanted to wake up tomorrow on her and Tom's wrought iron bed in their Berlin flat with white floorboards and watch him sleep for a moment, full of love for him. She wanted to spend the weekend walking through Berlin with Tom, winding through courtyards and alleyways, occasionally holding hands. She wanted Tom's stupid jokes and his kindness and to let him understand all the parts of her she'd kept hidden.

Cathy pushed her shoulders back and took a deep breath.

"You miss Jack, not me," Cathy said. "I never really loved you, I just felt guilty."

"You did love me. Of course you did," he said.

"The only reason we were together was because we both felt guilty," she said. "It was always about Jack. It was guilt, not love."

"That isn't true."

"You didn't answer the door when I came over the morning he died," she said without second-guessing herself or hesitating. "You only remember what you want to about that morning."

There was a pause as those words sunk in: a strange, black hole sort of pause that could have moved in various different directions. She could hear creaks in the museum, a car horn in the city beyond, an ambulance roaring. His eyes flashed. He inhaled, his body tensed and he took a step back from her. Her chest tightened with the memory of all the other moments in her life, just like this one.

"I didn't ever love you," she said.

With a familiar blinding crack her head reared back into a wall and she dropped the Oxo Cube box. It clattered onto the floor. She'd asked for it. She knew the buttons to press. Cathy had a sense of time protracting, a slow motion flash going off. The brave child inside her shielded its little face and curled up tight to fade away. The teenager gasped and the adult blanked out, unconscious on the floor of the coral storeroom. There was a point when memories become stories. The life he was dredging up seemed so far away and yet so intimate.

The aim of the early morning beach-combing missions with Jack was that the first haul was often the best. Flip-flops and trainers. Colourful ammunition cartridges. Lighters. Cleaning fluid from cargo ships and trawlers that they knew not to touch. Cathy did a cartwheel in the marsh that morning, leaving fingerprints in the mud. She had gone swimming, leaving Jack with her clothes on the beach as she often did. It was no big deal; she swam in the sea all the time without incident and he never went in without Daniel being around. She'd jumped the waves then dived right under and was hit by the salty adrenalin that only comes from holding your breath under cold seawater. She surfaced once, spitting and blowing snot out of her nose, then waved at Jack, who was just visible waiting for her on the beach as he always did. Seagulls had patterned the sky above his little silhouette, dipping in and out of the cloud. They were already screaming at the rising sun when all of the other birds began to wake up. Cathy had dived under again and suddenly the texture of the water changed. Something tugged at her middle and wouldn't allow her to surface. She had opened her mouth to shout, then inhaled water and was dragged down.

She nearly drowned that morning. She wasn't sure how she didn't, but she was a strong swimmer and probably remembered to swim sideways rather than against a rip current. She remembered surfacing and vomiting. The beach and the bridge and the houses had all been sucked up inside a thick mist by then, the way that a dream fades when you try to recall it. The marsh had simply disappeared into the sky. She shouted Jack's name but nobody replied as she began to swim towards the beach and then climbed up onto the sand, throwing up in the waves again. She walked shakily to where she guessed she'd left Jack with her clothes and hoped he would be waiting for her. She shouted again, but he still didn't reply so she assumed he'd got scared when the mist came down over the beach, and that he'd gone home without her. He was scared of the dark, and tides, and being on his own. Cathy found her clothes where she'd left them and walked away from the beach.

The morning Jack drowned she'd left the beach hanging with mist and quiet. A crow flew out of the haze and made her jump, a foot in front of her, before slipping away again. Mist was creeping amongst blades of grass as if it were just rising dew, only it appeared to be falling out of the sky. Something had crunched under her foot, a snail perhaps. She tripped over a sea heather bush and landed on her knees in the thistles, scraping the palms of her hands. She vomited seawater into the scrub again and tried to count her steps to calm herself down. The gulls were too loud and she had a feeling that the water was following her, ghost water, chasing her ankles and wanting to climb down her throat into her lungs again so she couldn't breathe. The tides were hounding her, scheming to fill her up and drag her down.

She banged on Daniel's chalet before going to bed, asking if Jack was in his bedroom, but her memories were unclear. She could have sworn she heard Daniel moving around in the chalet and a tap running. She cried on his doorstep and threw up in a bush next to his door, then figured Jack must be in there with Daniel after all, so she'd crawled dizzily into bed and fallen asleep while Jack, out there in the sea, was trying to save her.

⚜

As soon as he hit her Daniel took three steps backwards, towards the door, and stood as far as he could from her still body. She had an insolent, sanctimonious expression on her face and he regretted it, as he always used to. Her expression was almost triumphant, as it so often had been in Essex. *You didn't answer the door when I came over,* she'd said. *I didn't love you.* White light had exploded in his head.

The past was not how he had left it. He had buried something precious in the sand and now he'd dug it up the gift wasn't the same as he remembered. It was always, always Cathy who made him lose his temper. In prison he'd actually felt calm a great deal of the time, particularly after he stopped sending her gifts. He was known as a steady and reliable sort, except for one time when some kid stole the only picture he had of Cathy. Daniel should have just knocked the guy around a little and taken the picture back, but instead he'd lost his temper. He'd seen Cathy's face in the white light as he ruined the man's shins and jaw.

He hoped it would rain soon and the humidity would break. He bent down next to her and put his fingers on the pulse in her neck, which was strong. She'd be fine. The first time he'd ever knocked her out, back home, he'd been terrified she wouldn't wake up and checked her pulse every ten minutes, putting a jumper under her head and cold water on her forehead in an effort to bring her back. He had been about to call an ambulance when she'd resurfaced of her own accord and walked off in a daze to her father's chalet. He wished he wasn't near her now. He'd thought so much about the moment he would see her again, but it wasn't anything like what he'd expected. He was frustrated and told himself to take a deep breath and calm down. *I didn't ever love you*, she'd said.

Cathy's head lolled to the side so that one cheek was pressed against the floor, near to where she'd dropped the Oxo Cube box. Her mouth was open an inch and sweaty strands of hair stuck to her temples. Her arms were limp by her side and the strap of her dress had slid off one of her shoulders. He tightened his fists and dug fingernails into his palm, trying to count backwards, but he couldn't concentrate. When they were together in Essex he used to think about her breath all the time; its regularity, its speeding up when he was near, how easy it would be simply to make it stop and end their history at its source. She was so tightly knotted and inescapable inside his head, the origin of all his sadness. He stood with his back to the wall and held the counter. It would be a mistake to walk over to her now and put his fingers on her neck but it would not be an isolated, pivotal error of judgement. It would be intricately mapped to other *almost*-moments during their time together. The past and the future were in their blood and their brains. It all existed and it was simultaneous, real as the anger in him now.

She was still out and hadn't moved since she fell. Now he decided to leave the room and calm down, away from her. When her phone vibrated in her bag he reached to silence it. The screen said 'Tom'. He removed the coral storeroom door key from the inside lock and ran his fingers over its tip. It felt like a tiny cityscape. He held his lion mask in his hand and left the coral storeroom, breathless at the sight of her lying there on the floor. He'd come back when he had a plan. If something was going to break before this humid night was over, he needed to make sure it wasn't him. He slipped out of the door and locked it behind him.

⁂

Tom pulled out more cabinet drawers. He touched travertine rock from the Getty museum gift shop in Los Angeles and a small gold Buddha. He opened up the map of Berlin they'd used when they first arrived, with its circles and arrows and routes marked in various coloured biros. He'd drawn a picture of Cathy's profile across the centre of the city, over the *Tiergarten*, with the tip of her nose at the Brandenburg Gate. She had some of his tarot cards from ages ago, and a green cocktail umbrella he recognised although he wasn't sure why. Tom opened all of the cabinets and pulled out the drawers indiscriminately. There was the heel from a red suede shoe and a green shell next to ancient used Paris Metro tickets. There were shells and toys. Tom was overwhelmed.

His precise, orderly girlfriend collected knick-knacks and souvenirs. He wanted to give her a kiss, observe her face clouding sulkily when he told her he'd found her collection. He didn't care if she was angry with him.

He picked up a fading photograph of a sandbank in the sea at sunset, with what was perhaps a factory or even a castle silhouetted on the other side of the water. Shell made her childhood home sound much uglier than it appeared in this faded photograph. She said she had no good memories of Lee-Over-Sands, so she would never take him to visit the area where she grew up. The landscape was desolate, sure, but beautiful. It was unnerving to see a picture of a past she'd never chosen to share with him. There was also a photograph of Yellow Horned Poppies reaching up high from a bed of shingle while bright purple Sea Lavender kept close to the ground. A dozen of the snaps were of Cathy herself, although none was full-length. She was fragments and body parts in this collection, freckled white hands with scuffed knuckles, a ring made out of a shell on the middle finger; a toe, a mouth, the lined palm of her hand. Fingers on a thigh, a hand cupping a shadow between open legs, then – out of place – a dead heron photographed on a mud bank.

What's your favourite bird, he remembered Cathy saying a few weekends ago in their empty flat with wooden floorboards.

The Jeholornis, *an ancient Chinese bird with two tails. You?*

The heron. I like the way they move.

Do you have happy memories from being a child? He'd tucked hair behind her ear.

Sure, some. You?

Tell me one.

I always won the sprinting competition on sports day. My mum used to let me help her bake cakes for the local teashop before she left. My dad would take me bird watching. That's three. He had kissed the end of her nose. He hadn't known she collected Polaroid photographs or dried flowers.

Tom took particular notice of a Polaroid of a broad-shouldered man with a long, beakish nose and curly black hair. The man was standing in a river or estuary, smiling at the camera with an expression that could only be the result of loving the photographer. Tom considered this image, holding it at different angles and in different lights. The man had grey eyes and a bruise on his arm. Tom forced himself to look away from the photograph.

He had been so pleased by how much she'd opened up since they moved to Berlin, but perhaps it was all in his head. Maybe he'd spent the last years loving someone who was still a stranger to him. He picked up a photograph of Cathy's hands from the cabinet, her bitten-down finger nails covered in chipping teenage polish. The earth's atmosphere at ground level exerts a pressure of about fifteen pounds per square inch. We don't notice because the pressure inside us balances itself to equal the pressure outside us. A whale doesn't feel the water pressing on it at many tons per square inch. The shape of a bird's wing is designed so that as they move forward through the air, the pressure above the wing is less than the pressure below. As Tom slipped out of the office, he felt as if his pressure had been messed with and he was floating.

Daniel had left Lee-Over-Sands the same week Jack drowned. He'd abandoned the chalet, then later sold it for next to nothing and acquired a nasty debt to Marcus in the process. Daniel began driving lorries for Marcus to pay off his debt. Daniel hadn't been able to face his parents, so slept where he could for months. He liked the driving, spending long periods of time alone driving across the country and sleeping in his truck. He was aware that he was not only driving factory machinery and car parts across borders but the danger of being in charge of illicit cargoes appealed. Later, the money did too. He tried not to think about Jack's death. He did not go to the memorials his mother held every year. He continued boxing, making some money out of a renewed anger in his gut, but however hard he punched he still missed the way Jack lined up his pebbles on the kitchen table and picked the blueberries out of his blueberry pancakes. Daniel never ate blueberry pancakes after his brother died, and even the sight of a few pebbles or shells in a row made his palms sweat a little. He'd made a great effort to push thoughts of Jack away over the years.

When Daniel came back to Lee-Over-Sands it wasn't because of Jack and certainly wasn't because of Cathy, but just because he needed to keep his head down for a while and Lee-Over-Sands was at least good for that. The haulage company had got into trouble. Daniel wasn't privy to the details back then, he just knew he had to make himself scarce. He didn't rent the chalet he used to own, but instead a moss green one in the centre of the street. He found he'd forgotten many things about the area, like how a crust of scum formed at low tide where the water lapped the mud.

He'd been surprised by the limpness of the chalets and how the humidity rested on your shoulders even on a cold day. He didn't for a moment think that Cathy or her father would still be living in the same crumbling street on a sinking coastline. It was low tide the afternoon he returned and Daniel looked through binoculars at three oyster farmers collecting shells out on the beach in their galoshes, an old man throwing sticks for his pit-bull. Daniel swept his lenses over the horizon, a shaky line in the shaky rain, and paused over a figure of a girl. He put the binoculars down again, orientated himself and lifted the lens a second time to watch Cathy on the marsh. She bent down to pick something up from the ground, then lifted her own binoculars to the sky. She swung them along, following the path of an eagle above her. Daniel did the same and then considered turning away before she saw him.

Daniel was sure, even from half a mile away, that she took a deep breath the moment she saw him; whether it was from recognition or curiosity he wasn't sure. She stopped with her shoulders facing away from the sea and her binoculars facing his. Guns raised across enemy lines. The air tightened and colours were sharper. They both dropped their binoculars from their eyes and she began to walk forward away from the sea, directly across the low-sludge of marsh water and estuary water towards his chalet while pulling her rain hood off and raising her head up at him with those unexpectedly blue eyes.

Her hair was long like her mother's used to be and far darker than it had been when she was a child, sodden, perhaps, with rain and sea air. The thousands of freckles that used to make a constellation on her face had faded to just a scatter across her nose and cheeks. She appeared young and old simultaneously. Her face was insolent, with thin lips and skittish eyes that were much brighter, now, than when he'd first met her. It wasn't a pretty face. She had an alley cat look to her and he immediately disliked her for having stayed all these years, felt ill that that she hadn't left this nightmarish and lonely place with its crusts of scum.

You're back, she said, simple as anything, head tilted up and nose shiny with rainwater, like she'd merely been waiting for him to get back from a weekend away. He was surprised to be recognised. She'd only been a child then.

Not for long, he replied. *Just a week or two.*

Strange choice for a holiday. Shall we have a cup of tea? She crossed her hands over her chest.

I haven't been shopping.
I have tea, she said.

She kept her hands folded over her chest and he put on hiking boots to follow her down the street and into her chalet at the end of the road, nearest the bird sanctuary. As soon as he walked through the peeling blue door into the smell of space heaters and gin he knew it was dangerous to have come back. He hadn't realised how much he'd missed it there and how much it meant. Every surface of Cathy's house was still covered in shells and stones, although now there were cheap gold hoop earrings and eye shadows mixed in amongst her bowls of frosted sea glass.

The chalet's kitchen linoleum curled upwards at the edges with black muck in the crevices between tiles. The gas hobs were filthy and empty bottles filled rubbish bins as well as lining windowsills, decorated with dried marsh weeds and flowers. He saw through an open door that her bed was still the same bunk bed she and Jack used to play on; she'd just removed the top level. A black uniform with a white name tag on it lay crumpled on the floor next to the bed, maybe from the pub in town. Other surfaces were covered in papers and biology textbooks. Daniel could hear a man snoring behind the closed bedroom door, presumably Cathy's father.

Daniel's palms sweated as Cathy put the kettle on and began to heat up cinnamon buns in the oven. She had a greasy bag of them and they looked stale. There had been many girls before Cathy, of course, too many in the years of trying to escape himself, but nothing that he couldn't walk away from easily. He'd never been in love. Staring at this girl as she put stale cinnamon buns in an oven he remembered her mother used to make fairy cakes, he found it difficult to breathe.

Where's your mum? he said shakily as she passed him a cup of tea. He wanted to ask how she'd been, why she hadn't left the area, if she still ever thought about Jack, but he didn't. Words didn't seem easy.

Escaped to Majorca.

Majorca?

She's married to some Spanish hotel owner and she has her own bakery near his resort.

You don't see her? Daniel asked. Cathy was speaking calmly, but he could see that it hurt. Daniel had never liked Cathy's mother much, but it seemed appalling that the woman had left her daughter there on the edge of the world.

No, but I suppose we weren't close.

And your dad?

Cirrhosis of the liver. He's asleep right now.

Sorry.

He saw a bowl full of tiny plastic Micro machine cars and a windowsill decorated with an army of plastic soldiers, some melted together into patterns of limbs and heads. The sight of them made his shoulders tense. He hadn't thought about those toy soldiers for years, those elaborate beach fires. He used to love going out onto the beach with Jack and Cathy to watch objects melt, particularly enjoying how the toy soldiers would pucker and almost throb, before relaxing into each other and merging. There were also a few lead soldiers, including Jack's favourite, the one with a red jacket and a pointy hat. Daniel picked the lead soldier up, then realised abruptly what it was and put it down again as if stung.

Are these . . . Daniel couldn't finish the sentence, and his voice closed up. It made his head pound.

I'll put them away, she said, looking stricken. *Sorry.*

Grief does not evaporate. Cathy's face in the murky light made him think about how Jack would always *not be there*, through all actions and situations. It all flooded back to him as he looked at her, all the grief and guilt that he'd tried to suppress for the last years. Jack would never drink cold beer, sleep in the pressed sheets of a hotel bed or look back on old photographs. It now also occurred to Daniel that Jack would never see Cathy, nineteen years old, smiling tentatively with her hands on her hips. Jack would have loved to see her now. The absence of Jack was similar to fear; it flushed Daniel's veins with blood and adrenaline, yet standing in Cathy's kitchen he had the distinct sense that Jack was there, in the room with them. Daniel had felt a white heat in his head, but also as if he'd arrived home. Daniel, quite abruptly, wanted to reach over and touch the girl. When Cathy passed him a cinnamon bun on a plastic plate with roses on the rim, Daniel had tears in his eyes and had to turn away.

Tom stepped outside the museum's front door to light a cigarette, simultaneously checking his phone to see if she'd called him back. It was a quarter past eight and the prize giving was at nine. He called her phone again: it went straight to voicemail. Tom wasn't sure if he felt angry with Cathy or just confused by her collection of autobiographical keepsakes. Sometimes he thought he was just about to figure her out, then he'd discover there had been some fundamental mistake in his thinking, like getting the first word wrong in a crossword and having to rub the whole thing out to start again.

Tom hoped Cathy wasn't at a bar somewhere now, with that strange nocturnal look on her face. He called her yet again and when she didn't pick up he made his way out of the museum onto *Invalidenstraße* where roadblocks and construction machinery were left out in the street ready for the next morning. He stepped into the Mercure Hotel, a taupe building he'd never been inside before. The nearly empty bar smelt of air freshener and he stepped back out again. Clouds were gathering in the sky. He did a loop of the streets near the museum, peering into smoky hostel bars, Italian restaurants, and newsagents with men drinking beer on the pavement. He had an idea and turned left onto *Chausseestraße*, where there was a gate under an illuminated green sign for *Ballhaus* Berlin, one of the city's old dance halls. He'd been there a few times with Cathy to watch elderly couples tango in the century-old room under vast chandeliers, and the last time they'd gone they'd tried to foxtrot.

I can't believe you know how to foxtrot. You're totally ridiculous, Cathy had said as he tried to lead her, without much success but with great amusement. Although he knew the basic steps they kept bumping into other couples and stepping on each other's toes, having to stop and say sorry or kiss her.

You have an unfair number of skills.

I'm really not very good at this, he laughed. *I did a class once. Foxtrot is F in the phonetic spelling alphabet, right?*

Alpha, Bravo, Charlie, Delta . . . what's E?

Elephant?

Echo. I wonder who invented it.

Someone called Mike, or Oscar, or Romeo or Victor?

They'd laughed together in the crowds that night. Elderly

people kept telling them that they made a perfect couple and wanting to buy them drinks. Tonight, though, it was still early and there was just one couple dancing, methodically, to the sound of a waltz, watched from the balconies by a handful of self-consciously retro hipsters holding mint juleps and genuine Berliners sipping white wine spritzers and draft beers. The music plodded on as if in a time warp and Tom stepped up a spiral staircase towards the balconies to make sure Cathy wasn't sitting hidden at a back table somewhere. An old man with a purple bow tie was reading a newspaper and a middle-aged couple were arguing, drunk in a way that suggested they'd been at it all day, but there was no Cathy. Tom bought a double whiskey with ice on the side and sat down for a minute. He listened to Waltz No. 6 by Chopin. The couple held each other stiffly as they shifted around the room, turning occasionally, not smiling at each other.

Tom walked back to the museum with the tune of the waltz in his head. Before he went inside he saw a dirty leg sticking out from behind a tree in the corner of the car park and stepped idly towards it. The protester's boyfriend hadn't appeared. She smiled up at Tom as he approached her. She was sitting at the base of a chestnut tree in her black bikini with his jacket over her shoulders. Ants were crawling on her sugar-covered toes.

"So my boyfriend hasn't turned up," she said. "Obviously. Has he called your phone back maybe?"

"Afraid not," he said. "You want to call again?"

"I'm far too busy giving the ants diabetes to see my boy-friend." She stuck her lower lip out sulkily, and blew air upwards so that her sharply-cut blonde bangs fluttered. "Twat. What's your name?" she said to him.

"Tom."

"I'm Iris. Like the flower. You look like you've seen a ghost."

"You don't look very happy either."

"That's because I'm half-naked in a museum car park and my boyfriend hasn't called me back," she said and blew air up from her mouth so her bangs fluttered again. "Covered in treacle. What's your excuse?"

"I don't have one," said Tom. They were silent for a moment. "I can go see if I can find some more suitable clothing from the lost and found, maybe? And I'll give you some money for a taxi."

"Really? That would be great. Can I come with, though? The ants are tickling."

Tom didn't relish taking this girl into the museum with him. Cathy must be at the party by now; he should go back before she got her award. He wouldn't mention that he'd found her objects, not until later. He didn't want to ruin her moment. But the oily teenager appeared so miserable and embarrassed, shivering in the car park, even with his jacket on her shoulders, that he couldn't abandon her.

Tom had been looking forward to going for a late dinner with Cathy after the party. He'd been looking forward to tumbling into the Turkish café at the end of their road, tipsy with champagne and all dressed up, to eat messy falafel sandwiches and laugh about their evening. He'd imagined Cathy's award on the table between them, their knees touching under the table, her fingers brushing lightly over his as they did occasionally, as if just to say hello. He'd imagined her makeup a little smudged, leaning over to wipe mascara from under her eyes, then walking hand-in-hand up their staircase to their creaking old bed. He now had the distinct feeling that this wasn't how their evening would be ending.

"First we need to clean your feet somehow," Tom said to Iris, looking around for the gardener's hose as she got up, wiping sugared ants from her toes and ankles.

❧

Flashes of light were moving around in front of Cathy's face and she saw that she was lying on the floor of a small room surrounded by ocean coral, at which point she remembered that Daniel had come back. She shivered and assessed her surroundings without sitting up. Along one wall was a large yellow cabinet containing bottles labelled as hazardous, and along the others were cabinets of endless coral: Blade Fire Coral, Spiny Flower Coral, Great Star Coral. The coral had similar patterns to human veins and tree branches. Most were white, as if carved from chalk, but some were red. The tap of the sink dripped in its corner and above it a window looked down on the museum's scaffold-lined courtyard, where builders had recently been replacing crumbling brickwork and painting window frames.

The ocean architecture throbbed because her head was pulsing. She carefully sat up and then got to her feet, holding on to the counter for balance. She took three steps forward and reached for the door, but turning the knob she found that it was locked from the outside. She rattled it weakly. Her limbs were so heavy that she had to sit down on the floor again. She usually knew what time it was, but now had no idea. She wondered whether she had missed the prize-giving already. She noticed that her phone was gone from her handbag, as well as Jack's toy soldier and all Jack's Oxo Cube objects. She

140

put her head on her knees and could still sense him in the room and on her skin, as if he'd left remnants of himself there.

It was supposed to be a basic fact of memory that emotional events have more impact than neutral ones, but her recollections of the morning they found Jack's body mostly consisted of odd details. She knew that before they found him a cartoon called 'She-Ra: Princess of Power' had been on the little television in their kitchen, an episode about a reluctant wizard and a magical tree. She had poured herself a bowl of Cheerios to get rid of the bile taste in her mouth but she wasn't in the least bit hungry. Jack had left some of his Micro machines and shark teeth in her bedroom when they'd been playing on her bunk beds the day before, all in the Oxo Cube tin. Perhaps they'd have a barbecue later, if he didn't have to go back to his parents. Cathy's mother was icing a lemon cake in the kitchen while these thoughts came and went. Daniel appeared at the door, and she told him that she and Jack had gone swimming, but Jack had come back before she did.

The next thing she clearly remembered was watching Daniel walking over the bridge towards the beach, then her father following a moment later. Vomit rose up inexplicably into her mouth and she let some of it spill out into her hands, then onto the table and into her bowl of Cheerios. She didn't know what she was scared of. A while later an ambulance appeared and couldn't get over the little footbridge, so the paramedics had to run over the marsh carrying their gear. Bright orange uniforms disappeared after Daniel and the park ranger.

Cathy's mum said that it was at around this moment that Cathy began to scream, at the top of her voice, making repetitive high-pitched animal sounds. She didn't remember it at all. Apparently Cathy knocked the kitchen table over and everything scattered across the room, but she didn't say anything, just screamed mechanically.

If she closed her eyes and dragged herself back to that morning, she could see herself standing calmly at her kitchen window observing Jack's parents step out of an old car on the dirt road outside the chalets, but she couldn't possibly remember seeing herself observing Jack's mother, bleary-eyed with wonky lipstick and a large nose like both her sons. Or the father, solidly built with curly hair. Later a policeman appeared holding one of Jack's trainers. The shoe was blue and white canvas with worn-out Velcro and biro doodles of stars that she'd drawn on them. The policeman plus Cathy and Jack's parents all congregated round the single wet trainer. She remembered Daniel standing a little way off, watching as well. If her mother was to be believed, these were all things that Cathy had been told later rather than what she'd seen in front of her own eyes at the time.

It was such a disorganised set of recollections with so many holes in it, quite unlike the solid and capable edges of her objects. After Jack died it was as if the fragments of sensory detail she'd experienced had been catalogued so illogically that the bits could not re-form coherently into a recollection. Shards of the day were in her mind's basement, shards in back rooms and north wings and south wings and storage cupboards, or with erroneous labels attached so she could not see the whole in any reliable formation. It was liquid, upended.

She wished she possessed memory in the same way she possessed Jack's spectacles or his toy soldiers. She would have liked to own the moment in its unified entirety, hold it and understand it from every angle, but the memories slipped into themselves and changed. She couldn't control it.

Her mother said Cathy had refused to eat for days after Jack died and they'd had to take her to the hospital. Her father said that Cathy threw up on her first day at the school she and Jack were meant to be starting at together, when the teacher read Jack's name on the register. She couldn't unpick her memory of the story from any separate event. She remembered that she wasn't invited to the funeral, which took place at a crematorium nearby. She registered that one day when she got home from school, Daniel's chalet had been emptied. He'd done so much work on it, it seemed like all he'd done for months was fix up the place, yet it was still a dump when he left it. Cathy's mother said he'd lost all his money when he sold it.

The deck doors were open so she climbed up and knocked on the glass doors, but he didn't look up, so she walked into his chalet without invitation. He was sitting in a rattan chair, which was one of the few bits of furniture left in the chalet. There was also a white garden table that Daniel and Jack had used as a dining room table, with the chairs Daniel had borrowed from the deck of a house three doors down. In the corner of the kitchen were a few pennies, driftwood, old newspapers, and a fork. On the kitchen counter stood Jack's favourite toy soldier, wearing a red jacket and black hat. The soldier stood up very straight. Cathy walked over to the soldier and picked him up.

The chalet was quiet. Water rustled outside. It was getting ready to rain and the air was wet like the inside of someone's mouth.

That was in Jack's pocket, Daniel said eventually, quietly, watching Cathy stare at the little soldier. She turned towards him and saw that Daniel had abruptly started to cry. That big man, who was always hammering and sawing things, always bad tempered, was in tears. It was nearly silent at first, but after a moment he was properly sobbing, his face all scrunched. She walked over hesitantly, still holding the soldier in her fingers, and she put her small arms around this man's big shoulders. Her own scrawny body had jumped with his gasping, giant boxer's shoulders throbbing with panicked child sobs that couldn't take in enough breath. Tears streamed down his cheeks. She gripped the soldier. If Daniel and Cathy were a species, that hug on the deck after Jack died would have been their shifting moment, their shared mutation. He didn't hug her back.

Take it, Daniel said of the soldier. *I don't want it.*

It was his favourite.

I know. I don't want to look at it. You should have to look at this.

Cathy felt sick.

Do you understand what you've done? he said.

I thought he was with you. I knocked on the door, she said.

He looked away and didn't reply.

And so the soldier entered her collection. We think of our body as a permanent structure, yet most of it is in constant flux, with old cells dying and new ones sneaking in to take their place. The cells of the stomach live for five days. Our red blood cells last around 120 days, dying exhausted after travelling 300 miles through the body's circulatory system. Even our skeleton is replaced every ten years or so. Some of the only pieces of our bodies that are thought to last a life-time are parts of the brain and the muscle cells of the heart. It's memories that give us the sense of a consistent self. The flashback of comforting a crying nineteen-year-old version of Daniel was a key part of Cathy's identity, although its existence gave her shivers.

Daniel stepped through a high-ceilinged room with stripped walls. Cathy was so different now, as if she wasn't the same girl he'd loved but some newer model of the same doll. He'd spent so long imagining the moment when he would come back and put his thumb on the corner of her lip. He wasn't sure he liked the person that she'd become but, even worse, he was reminded of the person he'd been when in in her presence.

The museum was a maze and he didn't know where he was. He probably wasn't in the central wing any more, because he couldn't hear the party at all. Every room he entered seemed to have several entrances and exits, the main rooms all interconnected with archways rather than doors. He made his way through a corridor where there were flashes of former opulence. Leafy mouldings criss-crossed the ceiling and met in knots of foliage near columns. You could tell that the walls and columns had once been painted bright colours, because occasional leaf murals remained in a faded green paint. Unlike the grand cathedral atmospheres of other museums he'd visited with her when they were together, this one seemed the sort where you might find a stuffed human or two lost in the back. He thought of Cathy's body and his, sewn together in a waltz or a fuck. His breath grew more even the further he was away from her. He tried to inhale deeply and swallow his anger. As he passed he touched a skull, perhaps of a rabbit or a ferret, that was sitting on a wooden filing cabinet, and visualised Cathy passed out on the cork floor. He thought of her white skin. Maybe he'd only come back because she was a kind of habit.

He exhaled and entered a room that immediately felt vast, although it was so dark he could hardly see anything. Daniel sat down on the floor in the dark and closed his eyes, put his head in his hands, and counted backwards from ten again so he could think. His heartbeat began to slow down. In the dark and the quiet he held the toy soldier up in front of him and opened his eyes. He could just see the outline and feel its edges. Daniel used to buy Jack soldiers from junk shops in Brighton and Clacton. He'd bought him gunners, cavalry, tanks, once a box full of Waterloo British infantry, and bags of Victorian sailors. They even had a favourite toyshop. They'd go there and then to TGI Fridays for ice cream. Daniel hadn't bought his brother this red one though, it must have been a gift from their parents or Father Christmas. Daniel remembered the shark teeth Jack collected on the beach at Walton-on-the-Naze, the most prized ones still impacted into their gums. He used to spend hours watching the little boy fill his anorak pockets with fistfuls of teeth and fossilised wood. Daniel would carry the anorak home over his shoulder and they'd scatter teeth on the kitchen table to count and sort them into matchboxes.

Jack's best shark tooth was an *Otodus obliquus*, shiny as black marble. Once he drew a map of all his favourite places around Lee-Over-Sands: the power station at Bradwell-on-Sea, the funfair at Seawick and the crabbing pier at Mersea Island, connected to the mainland by an ancient Roman causeway that disappeared at the highest tide. He drew Daniel's chalet once, too, with a stick-figure Daniel and a stick figure

146

Jack standing on the roof holding hands. He wondered where those things were now, if they were in Cathy's collection. Daniel wondered if there was a picture of Jack in her cabinet. Daniel had been so keen to forget that he didn't even have a picture of his brother. When Jack wore Daniel's tank tops they used to hang down to his knees and make him look like a miniature gangster; a picture of Jack in that top would mean the world to Daniel now. Later, when Cathy had grown up, she wore his shirts and they would look similarly huge, but her nipples would press out through the ribbed fabric. Daniel didn't mean that image to corrupt his thoughts of Jack. She always appeared in his mind when he didn't want her to. Daniel held the soldier tight in his hands. He could feel blood pumping behind his eyeballs.

He opened Jack's matchboxes one by one and pushed out the trays with his thumb. Cathy and Jack had always liked matchboxes; they were so well-suited to a child's hand. Jack used to keep all his shark teeth in 'Ship' matchboxes. In Daniel's collection one was full of shark teeth, another with small shells. The third, unexpectedly, contained matches, and Daniel skimmed a matchstick against the rough side of the box, surprised to see it catch light. He let it burn almost down to his fingers and inhaled the sulphur. The soldier flickered in front of him, glowing a shaky yellow. Around the soldier, pincer-shaped jawbones of bowhead whales grinned on wheeled trays. Giant rib cages, like great curved boats, rested on the floor. Rows of dolphin skulls were wrapped in plastic bags above him.

Daniel had sat at the back during his brother's funeral. He'd arrived as it was about to start and left just before the end, as the coffin disappeared to the sound of piano music Jack would never have listened to. It was held at a crematorium a mile or so outside Chelmsford in a small white room with salmon pink carpets that matched the pair of curtains drawn around the little coffin. Windows looked out on a manicured lawn and at the front of the chapel a photograph of Jack in his school uniform had been printed on a piece of card and displayed on what looked like an easel. There were maybe twenty people in the room, most of whom were his parents' friends. Daniel's mother wore a black skirt suit that she'd probably bought especially. She'd sobbed loudly. When she turned her head in profile, Daniel saw her face, dripping and melting, red around the eyes and nose, blotchy around the cheeks. Daniel's father sat completely still, with his big shoulders hunched forward slightly and head bowed. Daniel couldn't see his father's face during the service, but imagined he was staring at the floor trying not to cry. Neither of his parents read something or spoke to the congregation at the funeral; that was left to an official who had never met Jack but who had been told to say how good he was at science, how much he loved his parents, how very much he would be missed. His parents blamed him for letting Jack go out swimming, for not noticing that Jack had sneaked out, for not keeping his little brother safe.

Cathy had not been invited to the funeral. No children were there, which had made Daniel sad because it implied Jack hadn't been popular at school. As far as Daniel was concerned Cathy was the only person who understood the depth of loss that Daniel experienced when his brother died. The loss was just there, always, between them, in the sound of the water or the sight of Cathy's smile.

A Christmas Sweatshirt

IRIS FOLLOWED TOM through the side entrance of the museum and the sounds of the party became louder. They could hear laughter and jazz music. She'd cleaned her feet with the garden hose outside and now left wet footprints on the marble hall and the carpeted staff elevator.

They stepped into the cool stone-walled basement where he'd got dressed with Cathy earlier. The party noises became muffled, reverberating slightly against the ceiling. The corridors down here had concrete floors and low ceilings tangled with pipes, halogen lights and fuse boxes. There weren't many specimens in this area: a five-foot brown bear at the far end of the corridor had a dust sheet over his head like a wedding veil; some snakes were curled on a grey filing cabinet. The bear made Iris jump.

"I'm a vegetarian."

"Lucky you don't have to eat Yogi Bear."

"Doesn't it bother you, being surrounded by death?"

"Not exactly how I think about it."

Tom walked quickly, anxious to be rid of her before Cathy's prize-giving. He motioned Iris towards a staff bathroom. He opened the door to a small janitor's room containing two sunken floral armchairs and many dirty coffee mugs. He searched through a lost property box of socks, T-shirts, teddy bears and sunglasses. He picked out a Christmas sweater with black reindeers cavorting amongst snowflakes.

"Thanks for doing this," Iris said from the door. Tom turned to see her tanned body without its sugary costume, just the black bikini. She'd managed to wash most of the molasses off, revealing her dimples and golden skin and a tattoo of what was presumably an iris flower on her arm. He threw her a pair of pink leggings and the Christmas jumper. She put his jacket on a chair.

The shape of her face and body reminded him of his first-ever girlfriend, centre midfield on the girls' high school soccer team. He'd lost his virginity to Gemma in the girls' locker rooms after school, aged sixteen. She was married to a film producer now and they lived in Bel Air with their two children.

Iris began to pull on the leggings. He could see her reflection in the dark glass window. A hint of fleshy thigh, a belly button, as she wriggled into the leggings. She was miniature, maybe a foot smaller than him, and when he turned around again she had to tilt her neck quite far back to meet his eye. She didn't put the jumper on.

"That is *so ugly*," Iris said, holding it in her hands. She had an expressive face, each frown or smile or blush providing a theatrical illustration of her thoughts. Tom figured he was over ten years older than this teenager. She had a straightforward prettiness and shallow eyes. She knew how attractive she was.

"You're blushing," he said.

"That's the worst thing you can say to someone when they're blushing."

"Darwin called blushing 'the most peculiar and most human of all expressions'."

"I bet he didn't blush, then. I can't go on the train dressed in kids' leggings and a Christmas jumper."

"Says the girl who arrived at a party wearing a bikini and molasses? And I'm happy to give you money for a taxi."

"He's a proper activist, my boyfriend," she frowned, ignoring Tom. "He'd never get stuck covered in treacle outside some shit museum. He was put in a Tasmanian jail once for a protest against logging in the Upper Florentine Valley."

She still hadn't put the jumper on and her nakedness was giving the room a strange energy, expectant and lively. Her mouth reminded him of a small, coral-coloured drawstring bag. Tom was aware that she was standing too close to his body, but he didn't step backwards to make more space. They were within easy touching distance of each other. Her legs were slightly parted and her hands were on her hips. Her nipples were visible, tight bullets of flesh underneath the fabric of her bikini top.

"Put on your Christmas sweater."

"I don't want to put on the Christmas sweater." She smiled sweetly at him. At close quarters her breath smelt of bubble gum. She opened her lips a little.

"You don't want me, Iris, I promise. I very often talk about dinosaurs at the dinner table and do puzzles in bed and sometimes I forget to recycle. Often, I even forget to feel guilty about forgetting to recycle."

"You forget to *recycle?*" She gave him an outraged stare.

"I hide recyclables in the normal trash. Plus I'm ten years older than you and I've never been jailed for arranging protests in Tasmania, so put the sweatshirt on."

"Separate your phantom! And get over yourself." She laughed, but continued to stand half-naked in her leggings and bikini top, her mouth inches from his. He did not move.

"I will start to recycle if you put on the sweatshirt." He

could hear whispers and vibrations of the party above them. Perhaps Cathy would be looking for him up there, wanting to make sure he was there for her prize giving.

"Do you have a girlfriend?" said Iris.

"We're getting married."

"So you love her."

"Yes. Of course."

"Why?"

"What do you mean, why?"

"I mean why do you love her?"

"I just do."

"So you don't know why?"

"I love how much sugar she puts in her coffee," he said. "It makes me laugh."

"That's not really enough to get me to put on the Christmas jumper."

He could actually taste the bubble gum on her breath, not just smell it. She smiled. She was so entirely and simply existent in the moment. There would be no secrets in a relationship with her, no puzzles. He knew that if he spent just an hour with this bright-eyed teenager he would know almost everything about her. If he asked where she grew up she would tell him what boy band posters were in her childhood bedroom and where her first kiss happened and what age she'd been when her mother and her father divorced. It would all be clear. He briefly allowed himself to imagine putting his fingers down under the pink elastic of Iris's children's leggings and her tanned thighs parting a little. He imagined his fingers on her nipples and how smooth her skin would be.

"She brushes her hair one hundred strokes before she goes to bed every night and I love watching her." Iris wiped a rogue streak of sweaty molasses from her sternum, and then licked it off her finger. Her lower lip was shiny where she'd licked it. "When she laughs she gets a little line between her eyes," he said. "Her eyes are amazingly blue."

"Nice, but still no," Iris blew her fringe out of her eyes again, jutting her wet bottom lip from her mouth for a second to do so. He did want to lean forward and kiss her. He imagined the simple pleasure of it. The jazz music made distant, indistinct noises above him.

"She thinks she's solitary but she needs me."

"She's a loner?"

"Put on the sweatshirt," Tom said. "Please. She regularly takes my breath away."

"No." Iris turned her head slightly to the side, observing him.

"She makes me feel . . . dismantled," said Tom.

"Dismantled?" Iris thought about it.

"Completely. All the time. Like her hands, her tongue, her shyness and strength and humour, they're either going to ruin everything in my life at some point, or be everything." He felt breathless and his face was hot. "She makes me impossibly happy and oddly scared."

"Oh," said Iris. "I'll put on the stupid jumper then, I guess."

A moth appeared at the window where he was standing. It was trying to get in from the courtyard towards the light. Iris pulled the Christmas jumper over her head.

Cathy considered screaming out of the coral room window, but she couldn't make a sound. Daniel sometimes used to lock her in her bedroom when he went out to see friends or go to work. She would never shout or climb out of the window, but just sit tight and wait for him to come home, because it was easier in the long run. Outside the coral storeroom window, scaffolding tubes criss-crossed the Devonian rock and fossil hall on the first floor with timber boards that created corridors. Cathy's head was swimming as she opened the window. Cooler air touched her face and it occurred to her that it might be quite easy to climb out onto this scaffolding. She could see bike racks, rubbish bins full of broken bottles and cracked wood planks, a mire of smashed glass and magazines below. It smelt heavy and rotten out there. She knew she probably had a mild concussion so would have to be careful.

He used to make her feel so small and needy. She was glad he'd hit her just then, because until that moment there had been a flicker of need still inside her, an enduring child-Cathy who was drawn to Daniel and what he represented. The violence was a reminder of everything belittling and traumatic she'd left behind when she ran from him. He was not, and would never be, her home again. As she leant out of the window, she knew with absolute clarity that she did not belong to Daniel. She had loved him because she did not realise there was kinder love in the world and because she was scared. She did not want to be scared any more.

Cathy was already barefoot, her neat black heels and handbag on the floor. She would leave them there. She listened at the door and imagined she could hear footsteps outside; she pulled up her dress to above her knees and tied it there so it didn't get in the way. She placed one bare foot out of the window, then the other, and sat on the window ledge, her toes touching the scaffolding. She took a deep breath before slipping out of the window completely, getting into a crouched position as close to the building's wall and as far from the edge as possible. Her head was throbbing, and the humid air was fat with potential rain.

Cathy pressed her back to the building's wall. She felt lighter than she had done in a long time as she stood up and moved, quickly but steadily, before Daniel could appear in the storeroom again. She didn't mind heights, but sometimes when she was on bridges and the top floors of shopping malls, the idea of falling appealed to her. She tried not to look down through the half-inch gaps between the wooden scaffolding planks as she walked to the next set of windows, only to find they were both locked. If she fell now she'd be a sacrifice to Daniel's cruelty. And a puzzle: detectives would wonder why this girl with a badly hemmed second-hand dress knotted to her thighs had fallen from a museum window. She looked down. There was a nasty drop from where the scaffolding ended to the courtyard floor and she didn't want to risk jumping. Looking up towards the roof instead, she wondered if she could climb back in through one of the skylights. She hesitated for a moment, then began to climb higher and higher up the outside wall, scrambling quite easily on the metal pipes to reach the roof.

After Jack had died and Daniel left at the end of the summer, Cathy began to stay in when it rained and stopped riding her bike over the seawall at breakneck speed. The Monarch butterflies migrated south and the water swelled up from the autumn rain. After that summer, the wind clattering on her bedroom windows made her anxious, as did seawater gurgling in the old pipes. Everything from fox footprints in the mud to birds scattering from their perches on the telephone wires made the back of her throat ache with tears. She would be so *sorry* that the birds were frightened. The fierce, brave girl she had once been became frayed at the edges, worn as a pebble licked by the sea. She spoke less, ran slower.

Driftwood was never curled into the shape of celebrity faces or animals any more, as if the sea had run out of inspiration, yet she became more interested in keepsakes. She began ordering her previously haphazard collection of small important objects. An object that was redolent of her father was comforting, because the object did not stay out all night or fall over in the shower as her father was starting to do. Her mother's lucky rabbit-foot was comforting because it did not have changing moods, was not desperately sad one minute and hyperactive the next. After that summer her parents argued all the time and Cathy was convinced it was all her fault.

Cathy began to appreciate the certainty of solid things rather than the morphing excesses of the weather and peoples' emotion. When her mother came into her bedroom and said she was leaving Essex for a little while because she was unhappy, Cathy had just nodded, because it seemed reasonable enough. She didn't ask her mother to stay, because she knew her mother would say no. Cathy's mum gave her eleven two-inch-high ballet dancers that she'd played with as a girl. Cathy added the eleven dancers and her mother's lucky rabbit foot to her collection. Later, she added the empty blue bottles that had contained her father's Bombay Sapphire. She added newspaper articles about the night Jack died, and articles about the imaginary lion who escaped on Lee-Over-Sands the following year. She couldn't leave the house without at least one of the objects that had once belonged to Jack, his plastic watch or glasses or soldiers. The solidity of these mementoes calmed her down.

Her father always had schemes for things to buy or make. In another life he'd owned a chain of gift shops in Chelmsford, but he'd sold it when Cathy was a baby. After that he made bird-feeders for local markets and homemade beer for local pubs that didn't want it, hanging out in pool halls pretending he was a hustler and taking tourists on bird-watching tours. A *varied career*, her mother used to say, sarcastically. He was the park ranger for a while: that was the job of which he had been most proud, the two and a half years he spent sitting in the ranger's cabin talking to people about the birds they'd seen. He'd write a list of all the birds spotted that week on a white board placed outside the hut and update people on such things as the nesting ground of Little Terns. The last summer he was employed people kept finding him drunk in his boxer shorts in the cabin. Later, Cathy had to clean up his vomit and lock herself in the bathroom when he was in a mood, waiting for him to pass out so she could go to the kitchen and make tea.

Cathy had always thought her mother's superstition was an annoying quirk, but after the summer Jack died some of her mother's preoccupations rubbed off on her. Three seagulls flying together, directly overhead, became a warning of bad luck soon to come and Cathy would stand absolutely still waiting for another gull to join the threesome before she walked away.

Sparrows carry the souls of the dead. When a swan lays its head and neck back over its body during the daytime it means a storm is coming that evening. An acorn at the window will keep lightning out. It's bad luck to put a hat on a bed. If you say good-bye to a friend on a bridge, you will never see each other again. Three butterflies together mean good luck. A swallow abandoning its nest on your house means your house will burn. Step on a crack, break your mother's back. An older boy at school mocked her for not stepping on cracks and she punched the boy. She was expelled, and had to go to a school that was further away. She was convinced that she made bad things happen with her mind. When storms came and whipped up her imagination she'd get panicky, thinking that her imagination had generated the storm rather than the other way around. She felt she was magic.

She didn't mind being unpopular at school. She was used to being alone: collecting moths in jam jars and pinning beetles on polystyrene sheets didn't endear her to the cool crew. She took photos of herself with her Polaroid camera, sometimes just to watch how the new dimensions of her body moved, worried that childhood was slipping off her body like a snake's sloughed skin. Sometimes, when her fingers searched under the elastic of her pyjama trousers she was scared of the images that filtered into her imagination. Cathy's night thoughts as she became a teenager were not populated with other people's faces or bodies. In her fantasies she had only a sense of her own body floating in blank space. In one recurring dream her limbs were pinned down into mud and she was squirming in it, unable to see where she was, but terrified. Every time she woke up from the dream she was wet between her legs. In other dreams she was flying over the marshes, a cross between Peter Pan and a ghost, except that as soon as she realised she was naked, she would start to fall and the falling would be awful yet pleasurable. She would dream of the girls in high heels that Daniel used to bring home.

She would often dream about dead animals and being lost

on the marshes. Sometimes if she actually found a dead animal on the marsh the morning after one of these dreams, a dead swan or seagull, a fox or the licked-clean skeleton of a magpie, she would think of the animal as murdered by her messy thoughts.

She felt dirty all the time and as if there was no release for the trouble in her head. She would go out on the beach where nobody ever came and take off all her clothes, just to sit there in the cold and look at how her body was changing. She tried to encapsulate the moments with her camera. Her nipples doubled in size between the ages of thirteen and sixteen, but her toes didn't change at all. Her eyebrows lengthened, but her face was a half-inch wider when she was thirteen than when she was eighteen. She had Polaroid photographs of the arches of her dirty feet and her forehead, examining her body as an archaeologist would examine a skeleton: the scratch marks from walking and running; small white teeth, thin mouth, blue eyes that she could see were the brightest and prettiest thing in her face.

When Daniel came back she wouldn't call what happened falling in love. It was more as if they fell into a pattern they ought always to have been in. He encircled her and became her home. He came back and all the loneliness crumbled. It was accepted between them that they wouldn't talk about Jack. She'd put all Jack's objects away in boxes, all his micro-machine cars and shark teeth, because it obviously caused Daniel pain to see his brother's things. They bottled those feelings up. Cathy and Daniel never used to speak about that summer when their paths first crossed.

What Cathy hated about memories was how they changed. You'd think that once something had happened, its dimensions would be solid. Things happen one way, after all. There *are* facts and fictions, only it's difficult to hold on to the line when occurrences become memories. We see only splinters of our surroundings, portions that are later tied together to create the illusion of a scene. The story of our past is changed by the activity of seeing and recalling. Each time we remember an event it has the capacity to shimmer into something else. We remember the act of remembering. We remember what we tell ourselves. Remembering is an art, Cathy knew.

It took Cathy fifteen minutes to climb up onto the roof of the Berlin Natural History Museum that evening in her long dress with moth holes in the lining. She had to stop a few times, trying not to look down, but eventually managed to haul herself up over a stone frieze and onto the flat rooftop. She stood with her head in the Berlin clouds.

Insulated pipes snaked the rooftop amongst metal chimney tops and frosted glass skylights. Ledges of crumbling wall were decorated with old graffiti – a woman's eyes, an hourglass and a tag of indistinguishable bubble lettering. The botanists' garden of dahlias, daisies and herbs decorated one corner. In another some deck chairs were folded up and weighted down with cinder blocks.

In the windows of the hotel opposite the back of the museum Cathy could see a woman staring at the television while breastfeeding her baby, a man typing on his computer, a teenager arguing with her father, a fat man eating a hamburger. She imagined releasing the scream she'd felt in her throat since she opened the Kissing Beetle that morning. The tourists in their hotels would stop watching TV and feeding their babies and eating hamburgers, all turning to see a girl in an evening gown screaming on top of the Natural History Museum.

The jazz music stopped as Tom and Iris stepped out of the elevator. To escort Iris out of the front door would have drawn attention to her, but if he took her round to the back door he might miss Cathy's award, so he ushered her up to the balcony around the atrium so that he could look down at the party and locate Cathy. It was nine o'clock; Iris stood next to him wearing the Christmas jumper and children's leggings. The museum director was on the stage, adjusting his microphone for his speech.

"I still can't see Cathy," Tom scanned the crowd of donkeys, birds and zebras in evening clothes. At the back of the room a flash of green silk caught Tom's attention for a second. The crowd briefly parted, changing shape, but it turned out to be an old lady's emerald-coloured jacket rather than Cathy's dress. The *Brachiosaurus* skeleton loomed. It was almost as if each person had chosen the animal that most suited them, whether they were sheep or bears. Tom thought back to when he'd last seen Cathy that evening. A layer of sweat covered his body: he thought he smelt hormonal and as if he were an adolescent again. He wanted a cold shower, a glass of iced water, and to touch Cathy's shoulder. Perhaps she'd fainted somewhere in the museum, or she knew he'd gone through her objects and was avoiding him, or she was in a bar on the other side of Berlin and he wouldn't see her again until tomorrow morning.

If he could just touch Cathy, then everything would be all right again.

The museum party was getting louder and nobody stopped talking or laughing until the director cleared his throat and tapped the microphone to announce that the prize-giving was about to begin. Tom wiped sweat from his brow and neck. He could feel it collecting between his shoulder blades. The thin corridor they stood on was decorated with oil paintings and stag heads, creating hundreds of eyes staring down into the atrium below.

"We are a small planet tucked away in the corner of a galaxy amongst millions of galaxies," the museum director began, addressing the crowd of tipsy guests. "Natural history museums teach us the vastness of time and how little of it the human species has occupied. Our role over the last two hundred years has been to tell stories through objects, to allow the public to interact with their own history."

The director paused and touched his moustache. He had it professionally trimmed once a week, so it was said. From above Tom could see triangles of sweat on backs across the party. He could see bald patches and paper animal noses, but no Cathy. He dialled her number again, but her phone had been turned off.

"But we must also look to its future," said the director. "We must learn from yesterday's narratives and weave these stories into new visions of tomorrow. I would like to raise a toast to two hundred years of inspiration, science and magic. Happy birthday to the Berlin Natural History Museum!"

"Happy birthday!" the crowd echoed.

Tom badly wanted Cathy to be standing opposite him. He wanted to be in a flea market with her, looking through tat. He wanted to be in a park or a garden or an airport. *The biggest hailstone ever weighed more than 1kg and fell in Bangladesh in 1986*, he'd say to her if she were here now. *An individual blood cell takes about 60 seconds to make a complete circuit of the body*, she might reply.

Matches

A GUST OF air skimmed right over Daniel's head, making him start and turn to look up at the animal faces lining the walls. He lit another match and saw a tiny blue-feathered bird – a live one – moving its wings on one of the larger stag antlers, shifting its weight from foot to foot and tucking its wings closer under its taupe neck. It must have flown through an open window and got lost in the unusual heat, unable to work out how to get out again. The feathery knot of muscle flung itself full-pelt off from the antlers and down the corridor, drawing a thread through the dark corridor like a fish sliding through a slipstream. It hovered in the air at the end of the room as if waiting for Daniel to follow it and Daniel had a sense that the bird was deep in thought. Daniel didn't move. The match went out. He lit another, inhaling the sulphur and wood smell in the air. He knew the creature in front of him was a swallow. Hordes of these birds used to come to Lee-Over-Sands in the spring and dance on the marshes. The bird stared at Daniel.

One magpie was sorrow, Cathy's mother used to say. Two was joy. An albatross meant getting lost at sea and kingfishers meant getting your wish. Swallows, he remembered, were a symbol of re-birth. He held Jack's Oxo Cube box. He wanted to be on the beach with Jack, teaching his little brother to make a fire in the sand. Collecting wood, digging a ditch half way down the water's edge, lighting tightly coiled torches of newspaper to throw into the kindling. He thought of Cathy sitting on the coral storeroom floor where he'd left her, awake by now perhaps and biting her nails while staring at the door, digging under the corners of her toenails for the dirt that collected there at the edges every day. She'd be listening for creaks outside the door, waiting for him to come back, but he wasn't sure he wanted to be near her. The two swollen knuckles on his right hand were throbbing again. It would surely rain soon. He wanted to be in some wide-open space, as the bird probably did. He wanted to be alone and in control of himself, not close to Cathy and, because of her, lost in memories that hurt him. The swallow launched itself off again in the half-darkness. As it flew through a slim gap in a door and disappeared from sight, Daniel wanted the museum ceiling to dissolve and all the solid objects, the shards of bone and fossil, to splinter into a million pieces.

The bird had gone. Daniel moved into a room where a giraffe skin was hung up on a rail inside what looked like a half-open wardrobe. He lit another match to see it clearly, sliding the door a little further to reveal the skins of elephants and alligators, otters and seals, warthogs, gibbons and bats, all lined up as if they were costumes for a surreal theatrical production. Daniel blew out the match and continued with long strides in the direction of Cathy. He loved the smell of blown out matches. *You didn't answer the door when I came over,* Cathy had said to him. *You only remember what you want to.* As he walked down the corridor back towards the coral storeroom, he kept stopping to look at things, biding his time. He ran his finger along books and touched the tail of a stuffed fox. He needed to go back and check Cathy was okay, but he was reluctant. As he walked through the museum he imagined she would be sitting on the floor and he'd sit down next to her, lean against the wall, his knees and his head in his hands. He wouldn't touch her. He should never have touched her at all. He would turn towards her and be honest. He would look her in the eye and say: *I didn't answer the door and I'm sorry. There's nothing in the world I regret more than that moment.*

She would smile.

It wasn't your fault, she'd say simply. *We should forgive each other.*

He would like to be forgiven. The night before Jack died, Daniel had watched several films in his room: two Bonds, some porn. He was with a leggy girl who was smoking menthol cigarettes that night. The two of them had put Jack to bed, pretending to be grown-ups, then got drunk on cheap gin like the teenagers they were. They'd spent the night fucking and drinking and early the next morning Daniel had heard a noise at the front door that sounded like a fox scratching at the wood underneath the chalet. He went out into the kitchen, not so much to investigate as because it woke him up and he knew he needed a glass of water. He heard noises on the front stairs, but at that moment he was naked and stank of come and beer, so only looked through a window at her. Cathy was wearing a pair of tracksuit bottoms but no top, and her knees were hunched up to her chin. Her hair was wet like she'd just had a shower or been swimming and she was taking in hectic gulps of sea air with her eyes scrunched closed. Her face was blotchy from the tears. She leant over and banged at the door in frustration but Daniel didn't open it. He thought she must have had an argument with Jack - maybe this was what a lover's tiff looked like for ten-year-olds. She was the sort of kid who tumbled and screamed rather than fell and cried. Since he'd met her she'd fractured a bone in her foot from jumping off a wall, she'd had to be rescued from the roof of a derelict chalet while trying to save Apricot the tabby cat, who afterwards jumped down easily of his own accord, and sliced open her knee falling down on glass at the fairground where she wasn't allowed to go. Daniel hadn't wanted to talk to his melodramatic feral neighbour just then. After a few moments she appeared to get bored of sitting there making trouble, sniffed her tears away, and walked back to her own chalet. He'd never told her that he remembered this.

Now Daniel opened the door to the coral room, but Cathy wasn't there where he'd left her in the darkness amongst chalky white fingers of sea garden. He closed his eyes tight and felt his head swim with a feeling he didn't understand: he realised it could be relief. Her shoes and handbag sat on the cork floor and the window was open. It looked out on what Daniel now noticed was scaffolding erected around a small courtyard of skips and bike racks. Daniel touched pieces of coral in the otherwise empty storeroom.

He opened the yellow cabinet on the far side of the room and peered inside at plastic and glass bottles in all shapes and sizes, labelled 'Isopropyl alcohol', 'Ethylene glycol', 'Propylene glycol' and such. He picked out a smallish bottle labelled 'Ethyl acetate' that had a symbol of a flame on the bottle. He opened it and smelt the flammable kick of nail polish or glue. It made him think of throwing white spirit into bonfires to make Jack and Cathy scream on the beach years ago, all of them watching the flame leap up and eat everything in its path. Daniel put the bottle in his jacket pocket. He walked back out of the coral storeroom again with his blood pumping hard.

❧

Cathy took a few steps to an open skylight in the roof of the bird gallery. She peered down the hole into the room of stuffed birds. The ceiling was low, maybe seven feet above the floor. She sat at the edge of the skylight with her legs hanging inside the building, and then turned over so she was on her stomach with her torso on the roof, her legs still dangling inside. She pushed off and hung by her arms like a child jumping out of a tree. The jolt hurt her shoulders a little as she let go to fall barefoot on the wooden floors.

Cathy landed right in front of a cabinet of swans, bending her knees so as not to make too much noise. She immediately listened for any door hinges or floorboards creaking around her. Daniel was probably somewhere in these rooms. The air smelt just faintly of mould. She could hear music from downstairs, but not much else. When a swan flies against the wind, her mother used to say, it is a sign of rain. If a child sees a dead swan, the child will become ill. A single swan on a lake means death is in the air. Cathy stood absolutely still amongst the bored and glassy eyes of stuffed birds. A stuffed flamingo is an intensely sad thing and she tried not to look, but still imagined it wriggling awake on those long legs.

The music stopped downstairs and a microphone squeaked. She was not directly above the atrium, but could still hear the party. She guessed that this was the start of the prize-giving ceremony and it was a relief to have some indication of what time it was. She could still get there. She'd be a bedraggled sight with a thumping eye and no shoes, but it would be worth it. Aged ten, she didn't care what people thought of her: she could be that person again. She could collect a prize for research she'd work hard on. She could leave Daniel roaming this museum on his own; she didn't have to play cat and mouse with him. She could have a late night dinner with Tom at the Turkish café at the end of their road while people stared at them because they were all dressed up eating falafel with their fingers. She could begin to tell him about what happened to her. Her knee could touch Tom's knees under the table, her fingers brushing lightly over his just to say hello. Later she could watch Tom inhale cigarettes in the dark on the balcony of their apartment, and next week they could buy a cat, and next month they could get married. When she kissed him then, maybe there would be dust in his stubble and his eyebrows, thousand-year-old specks that had been eased from a mammoth tibia just like the first time they'd kissed in Los Angeles. Yet Cathy still had a bad feeling in her gut and she could have sworn she could smell the faintest hint of smoke, or burning, in the air.

She ought to have continued through the bird gallery and down the stairs, but instead she stood still and sniffed the air again just to make sure. Perhaps it was her imagination, adrenalin confusing her senses, but she could smell burnt-out matches and hot dust. Maybe it was just another alien stink sweating out of the walls in this heat wave, but it made her palms sweat. Nerves had always heightened her sense of smell dramatically. As she stood there she did not notice a blue-feathered swallow watching from the room's far corner. The bird swooped through the dusty air, neat as a paper airplane, to catch its breath in the opposite corner of the room.

Although Cathy felt a shiver, a twitch of moving air, she was distracted by the smell and remained unaware of the little flash of life in the museum full of death. She had a picture of the museum as an origami structure that was re-arranging itself while she was inside it and not letting her escape, while new doors were being created and corridors were stretching. She also felt as if she was being watched, but this wasn't unusual for her. Cathy would often turn a corner in this museum and sense she was being observed, only to see a stuffed polar bear or grumpy squirrel glaring from a doorway or cabinet.

She listened for the slow groan of cabinet doors or footsteps around her, attentive to any noise that might be Daniel in the shadows. Experimentally, just to put her mind at rest before continuing downstairs to collect her prize, she walked away from the stairs and instead in the direction of her office, to see if the burning smell would intensify or disappear. She moved through two more small rooms and into the corridor lined with warehouse shelving and the drawers of colourful birds' eggs outside her office. As she walked, the smell got stronger, a bit more chemical. Cathy felt sick, hearing her blood beating in her ears, and she didn't notice that the precise, almost mannerly, swallow had followed behind her in loops and dives.

The swallow flew with quick and stealthy wing-beats. It landed on shelves and cabinets between dives. The museum director was still giving a speech; she could hear muffled German and a squeaking microphone through the floorboards. She had time to run out of these interlocking storerooms back through the bird gallery onto the landing and down the stairs, then through the solar system and make it into the atrium for her prize, but she didn't move. Cathy heard an odd swish, a ruffle. The swallow knocked something off a shelf and made her jump. Her head throbbed, surrounded as it was by cabinets. The bird must have landed softly, because no noise followed the crash. She held her breath and waited for Daniel's breathing on her neck, or his hands on her shoulder.

Downstairs, the museum director stopped talking and Cathy found herself standing outside her office door. She thought of how Daniel used to love setting fire to her toys on the beach when they were younger, melting her dolls and turning toy soldiers into puddles. She closed her eyes.

All her scars tingled then, that little museum of experience on her skin. In natural history museums the whole bursting expanse of nature was boiled down into a story that you could walk through, room-to-room, creature-to-creature: butterflies born in the Amazon and pinned in Italy, which somehow found their way to Berlin, a rhino shot on the Indian subcontinent in the early nineteenth century and then skinned, stuffed and shipped to Paris, acquired by the Berlin Natural History Museum in 1910, swapped for a bald eagle and a pot-bellied pig. Same with a body: a bite on her thigh, rope burn on her ankles, a mark on her knuckles where the skin tore to the bone after he smashed it into a wall. The humerus bone in her arm, snapped from being pushed off the deck. The scar on her forehead from hitting her head on a window and smashing it. He'd driven her to the hospital and sobbed after that episode, bringing her hundreds of tulips over a series of days. She could have told someone then, but she didn't because she was weak and didn't know how she'd survive without him. Her body had healed; the feverish dreams of seagulls scavenging inside her head had subsided. She'd kept their world secret for such a long time. Her scars and her objects were all just stories now.

The smell of burning drifted in the air and she heard a noise coming from inside her office door. Music started up downstairs at the same moment, her chance to accept her prize lost now. She could taste his skin in her mouth from where his fingers had earlier touched her gums. She put her tongue in the gap where the molar used to be and inhaled the smell of burning. She stood very still outside her office, then pushed through the door.

❧

The birthday toast echoed amongst high ceilings, dinosaur skeletons and cabinets of gems. There was a wave of applause. Tom called Cathy's cell again, but it was still turned off.

"I'm extremely excited to be awarding the prestigious Loye grant to a young scientist with enormous promise," said the director, whom Tom thought had always had a bit of a crush on Cathy, "In order that she can continue her research into the retention of memory through metaosis in Tobacco Hawkmoths. Would Dr Cathy Miller please come and join me on the stage?" The room applauded.

Cathy did not appear on stage. She wasn't amongst the other entomologists, or in the huddle of scientists waiting to get their prizes. The applause died down and eyes began to rove the room. Tom and Iris stepped backwards in unison from the balcony edge, having shifted forward slightly to watch the prize-giving, merging with the shadows again so nobody could see up there. The hiatus continued an awkwardly long time.

"Does she have long red hair?" whispered Iris to Tom in the darkness.

Tom didn't reply to the question; after what seemed an age, the director made his apologies and continued on with the other awards. A microbiology professor went up, his face like bacteria under a microscope, a wildlife photographer marred by acne was next, a paleobiologist almost tripped over his feet on his way up to the stage.

"How do you know she has red hair?" Tom said to Iris.

"Wild guess, but I think maybe I saw her outside the museum earlier. She had her head in her hands and looked really upset."

"Why do you think it was her?"

"A hunch. She said it was the heat making her ill, but she looked scared."

"Scared in what way?"

"She looked pale and flinched when I touched her."

"She is pale, and most people flinch when strangers touch them."

"She flinched like she was scared of something. She was wearing a prim white shirt and grey trousers."

The jazz music started up again and Tom's phone vibrated. He fumbled too-eagerly to get it out of his pocket, feeling tension roll off him at the thought of Cathy's voice on the other end of the line. Instead it was a misspelt text from an unknown number, presumably Iris's boyfriend.

"I think it's your Tasmanian tree hugger," Tom said and showed Iris his phone. The party was suddenly back in full swing, drunk and loud, the prize giving finished. Iris wouldn't be noticed slipping out of the party now.

"She was scared," said Iris. "I liked her. I'm glad you made me put on the Christmas jumper."

It was a wet kiss that lingered, cool on his skin for the

briefest of moments and then evaporated by the time she'd turned away. Iris padded down the stairs and out of the museum's front door wearing the Christmas sweatshirt.

A Vertebra

Cathy's office was darker now, lit only by the moonlight coming through the windows. Daniel had struck a match as he approached Cathy's cabinet. He'd stepped into Cathy's office through the same door he'd left from earlier. He swung Cathy's cabinet door open wider and was glad to be here now, to have all her objects and catalogued memories to himself. The bottle of chemical liquid was weighing down his pocket, crammed in next to the raptor claw that he hadn't given her. He sat down on the floor and put the Oxo Cube box next to him. He took out drawers that contained objects from her life in Berlin, including photographs of her kissing her American, and sketches that looked nothing like her, except for a hint in the eyes. The first match burnt out and he lit two more. He pushed her objects roughly away, scattering them across the room. He took the rest of the drawers from the cabinet and arranged them on the floor around him. He picked out the objects he'd sent her: a coiled shell with glossy pink insides, the skull of a seagull, a fish spine, bird eggs, dried starfish, a fragile sea dollar, all things he'd imagined her loving and caring for. He took his time examining these objects, then he observed some of the objects that had been in her chalet when he'd first got back to Brecon, which she had put away so as not to upset him. Daniel unfolded a bunch of newspaper clippings from a yellowing envelope. Inside was an article with a picture of Jack in his school uniform, the same photo they'd used at his funeral. The photographer had obviously told him to smile, but he looked clownish.

Daniel slipped it into his pocket. He'd like a picture of Jack's grass-stained knees to keep or a recording of his voice carrying across the marsh, asking what was for dinner. Or a picture of Cathy and Jack on the beach surrounded by tin cans and bicycle spokes and teacups without handles and such. Daniel had been so happy then.

He picked up some Polaroids of Cathy's teenage body. He put his thumb on her freckled white hands and on her toe, then on a captured shadow between her open legs. With the dying end of the last match he'd lit, he thoughtfully set alight the corner of the photograph of her legs. It caught immediately, curling, letting off a rancid chemical smell, turning the Polaroid's edges into lacy ash before they disintegrated. The heat made the chemicals in the picture turn watery red. He wanted the stuffed museum alligators and birds she loved to decay, for the skeletons to divide from each other and the feathers to burn off the skin of all the dried-out birds.

He no longer wanted to be weighed down by Cathy's presence. He wanted all the misguided gifts he'd sent her to collapse into nothing, from shells to the Kissing Beetle. He wanted her mother's toy ballerinas to evaporate, the miniature glass bottles that had held Bombay Sapphire and still smelt of gin, the mouse skulls and dried flowers: he wanted it all to be far away. He thumbed the bottle of Ethyl acetate in his pocket, thinking of the pleasure he used to find in burning objects on the beach when Cathy and Jack were little, the stench of incinerating plastic and curling newspaper as they ruined dolls and cars together, sand spitting off the driftwood as it turned to ash and the toy soldiers became faceless. Daniel imagined pouring Ethyl acetate on Cathy's objects and throwing a match on top so the memories spat and collapsed into nothing, the fire spreading quickly through the museum from room to room. He envisioned the satisfaction of walking away while the museum flung smoke into the sky and everything Cathy loved was wrecked.

He didn't love her any more. As the photograph burnt away it was a revelation, or a punch, but it didn't feel like a surprise. It was more as if the realisation had finally wormed its way to the surface of his mind. He used the corner of the photograph to set alight one of Jack's toy soldiers. Not Jack's favourite soldier with the red coat, but a small khaki plastic one with an orange hat. The body morphed, the plastic fumed, then the body collapsed. As the soldier melted, the tight feeling in Daniel's gut disbanded slightly.

You didn't answer the door. He repeated the words in his head. That morning, before he'd found Jack's body, he'd gone to his room to wake him up, but his bed was empty. Daniel figured he'd gone to Cathy's for breakfast, so ate toast with strawberry jam on his own and watched *The Simpsons*. The girl he had slept with the previous night was snoring gently and dribbling on Daniel's pillow. After finishing his coffee and toast he knocked on Cathy's parents' door at the house at the curve of the estuary. He could see Cathy in her pyjamas watching a cartoon and eating cereal while her mother was making lemon cake in the kitchen. Cathy's dad looked even more hung-over than Daniel felt. Cathy had stared insolently at him for a moment, and then went back to the TV. Her dad said Jack hadn't come over for breakfast that morning.

Where's Jack? Daniel had said to Cathy. At that moment

he remembered the crying outside his door a few hours earlier but didn't mention it. *Were you with him?*

We went swimming but he came back ages ago, she replied.

Daniel had walked out onto the marsh shouting Jack's name. Cathy's dad came out with him and they walked in opposite directions. Daniel scratched an itch on his arm as he turned a corner past some rocks on the beach and in the early morning light saw a pile of clothes that had washed up there. Birds were dancing in the waves at the water's edge, playing chase with the sea foam. The air was cool. The sky was white. Getting closer, Daniel saw they were Jack's clothes - Jack's lurid green GAP sweatshirt, his stonewash jeans - and began to run. Up close, he found one trainer and two blue socks, one pulled down slightly over a bloated foot. The child's face was misshapen. Daniel wouldn't have recognised him if it weren't for the clothes. Daniel shouted for help and the words were sucked up into the empty sky and marsh around them. He had to shout several times before he heard Cathy's father's shout back. Daniel put his lips to his brother's lips and tasted cold seawater and vomit. Cathy's father must have called the ambulance, because eventually the noise of sirens mixed with the cries of the seagulls. Daniel kept doing mouth to mouth until it came. Cathy's father must have called his parents, too. When Daniel reached into his brother's pocket for some clue to what had happened he only found Jack's favourite lead toy solider in there. His parents wouldn't let him ride in the ambulance with his brother's body after he was pronounced dead.

One of Jack's wet trainers remained on the floor next to the ambulance tyre marks; it must have fallen off when they took his body. It had Cathy's scribbles all over it, which had made their mother angry a few weeks ago. They were blurred from the seawater. Daniel's parents had gone to the hospital, but they'd told Daniel not to come. Daniel was nineteen and his whole world changed in that moment. He'd been hung-over after a night of gin and porn while his baby brother drowned.

As the soldier descended into a puddle of plastic limbs, the flame weakening, Daniel heard a swish of air in the room and looked up to see Cathy standing there at the door.

⚜

Tom marched through a gleaming steel taxidermy lab. In huge silver tanks around the corners of these high-tech rooms, animal bones were exposed to enzymes that stripped off flesh, finely timed according to the size of the skeleton. A pelican was being restored on the sideboard, the shrunken skin on his neck revealing stitches and stuffing. An elongated penguin sat in the middle of the room, assembled by someone who'd clearly never seen a live penguin.

"Cathy?" Tom shouted, but got no reply.

He opened the doors to a room with four rhino horns peeking out from wooden crates. The rhinos had been removed from the public displays downstairs because of a spate of robberies in Europe that summer.

The scientific name for the Indian rhinoceros is Rhinoceros unicornis, Cathy had said the other day, looking at the ponderous expressions of the rhinoceros heads trapped amongst filing cabinets. *They're unicorns.*

Fat and wrinkly unicorns. The creatures all had wrinkled frowns with worried overbites, boxed up in here amongst filing cabinets.

Don't be cruel. Don't you think they've been through enough?

The rhino heads looked sly today, as if plotting their escape from this dusty former registrar's office. Tom crossed over a skinny yellow corridor where all the doors were closed except one. It was about halfway down the corridor and wide open.

"Cathy?" he said.

Nobody replied, so he walked towards the door. Inside the coral storeroom, Cathy's high-heeled shoes and handbag were on the floor as if she'd spontaneously combusted. The window was open, facing out on the trash-filled courtyard. Tom panicked and shouted her name out of the window. When he heard no reply, only traffic and distant party music, he eased himself up onto the counter and climbed out onto the scaffolding. He put his feet on the wooden base of the scaffolding and stood up.

He shuffled along the ledge and tried to get in through each of the windows that overlooked the courtyard, but they were all locked: either she'd climbed back in through one of them and locked it behind her, managed to make it down to the courtyard, or scrambled onto the roof. Below him the ground was mossy with dandelions springing up in the corners where the window glass met the brick. Tom could see the glint of a few bikes against racks on the far side, but mostly the space was filled with numerous trash cans and skips. Bricks and pieces of wood were piled against the wall amongst bottles of paint thinner and cans of paint. There was a full moon which, together with the city lights, illuminated his walk. The air smelt of the methane and rotten eggs coming from the rubbish bins.

"Cathy!" he shouted.

He figured she must have climbed down into the courtyard

and walked round the museum to the front. There was a worryingly big drop between the scaffolding and the floor, which he only just negotiated without hurting himself. If she'd jumped down like that she might well have a sprained or broken ankle. He trudged round the side of the museum. Guests were still smoking on the front stairs at the and drinking champagne underneath the *Brachiosaurus* skeleton inside. Instead of mixing with the party he took the elevator up to the top floor. He didn't want to talk to Jonas the guard. Tom picked up the atlas vertebrae of a horse as he made his way through the museum. Twenty-four vertebrae make up a horse spine, a human's has thirty-three. Seven cervical, twelve thoracic and five lumbar, all heavy industrial names for fragile lozenges of bone that we share – give or take – with snakes and dinosaurs, owls and chameleons. Most people assume bones are inanimate parts of their bodies, but in fact they are just like museums or cities, just like hearts and skin, constantly changing and marking the passing of time. A bone's exterior shape tells us about the animal's anatomy, growth rings show the climate the animal lived in, the microscopic structure provides clues to the animal's metabolism. Tom was about to walk into Cathy's office when he heard voices inside, so instead looked through the glass panels in the doors.

Cathy's body language was both familiar and different. The man with her was pale, his body language aggressive: Tom recognised him from the smiling Polaroid image in Cathy's personal natural history museum. Tom wanted to burst in, to do something absurd and heroic, to break the tension, to reach out and touch her, but instead he held onto the bone in his fist and watched through the panelled glass.

Cathy had opened her office door and stepped forwards. Daniel was sitting on the floor surrounded by her objects. The air smelt of burning plastic. Her knees were shaking and she could feel her pulse in her fingertips, neck and even her eyelids. Her memories were bubbling and reconsolidating so she was losing moments of the present, savouring a taste of salt, a texture in the clouds, a word here and a smile there. She could see a burnt photo beside his knees. She could almost feel the memory traces forming new patterns in her head.

They'd fucked against the frame of the peeling open window of her bedroom the afternoon before she'd finally managed to leave Essex, her lungs filling with marsh air. Daniel had tried to force her head further down so her body would be ninety degrees over the window ledge and her head thrust outside into the marsh air, but she had held herself upright in a way she would not have normally, with her arms and elbows against the window frame. It had hurt to keep herself from bending over while he pushed her, but she hadn't wanted to be pushed down anymore. She hadn't said anything, she'd never expressed herself with words. Instead she'd just disappeared in the middle of the night and reported him to the police.

Now she watched Daniel with her objects spread around him. She felt history falling. Scattered near Daniel were her auk and gannet skulls, exotic shells, toy boats and seabird feathers, all in the wrong places. She should not have let him handle these emblems of the past that she'd put so much effort into cherishing all these years. She shouldn't have allowed him to reach inside her mouth with his dirty fingers and touch her missing tooth. It was weak of her.

Daniel lit another match and smiled at Cathy. His papier mâché lion mask also appeared to smile in the darkness. The flame wavered.

"What are you doing?" she said.

She could see his knuckles, illuminated by the flame, turning white. The flame gobbled up the match and slid close to his fingers. He blew it out at the last minute and smiled an adolescent smile at her. Objects were jumbled together on the floor without any comforting gaps between them. The spectacles and the matchboxes of shark teeth, the little cars and toy soldiers scattered amongst shells and ballerinas. Dried flowers from Los Angeles with broken petals sat next to Tom's sketches and Jack's green plastic cars, nothing in the correct order any more.

"Do you think Jack would have worked in a place like this, if he were still alive?" Daniel said.

"He wanted to be a racing-car driver."

"Of course."

"But he could have been a scientist."

Daniel put his thumb on the face of Jack's broken plastic wristwatch. She was surprised that the watch didn't begin to tell the time again, immediately, the moment that Daniel's touch came into contact with the plastic.

"We used to pretend we could make all the birds and tides pause with it," she said. "He loved that watch. He used to say 'my brother gave me this watch'. "

"I made that extra hole so it fit his wrist."

"He loved you. You were a great older brother, I was so jealous that he had you."

"He used to get this blissful look when you were nearby, even so."

"He hated that I didn't organise my objects properly. All my things were jumbled up together then, do you remember? He used to sit on the deck and sort my objects into categories. Shells, mum, dad, insects, bones."

"He would have liked this collection."

"Or sometimes he'd sort them out by the date they entered my collection, beginning with the mouse skull from the start of the summer."

Cathy took a step further into the room as Daniel picked up the mouse skull that she was referring to. He held it up.

"This one?" he said.

"Yeah. I spat at Jack, remember? Right between the eyes."

"He told you your breath stank."

"I'm sure he was right."

"Personal hygiene wasn't your strong suit."

"He got dimples when he laughed."

"His feet were crazy ticklish."

"He was happy before it happened," Cathy said. "We had fun collecting stuff on the beach that morning. You were going to take him to the toy shop the next day on the way to your parents and buy him some more soldiers," she said. Daniel shook the matchbox and took out another match. She watched him scratch it along the side to coax up a flame. It fizzed and then straightened and he held it near the mouse skull. "Put it out," Cathy said. "There are five hundred people downstairs."

He let it burn to his fingers and then, smiling at Cathy, blew it out.

"He would have wanted you to be happy," Cathy said.

Daniel didn't smile.

"I should have burnt the whole chalet down when you left me."

"I shouldn't have stayed as long as I did."

"I burnt your text books and pieces of driftwood, your dolls and trainers and clothes and all those feathers you used to collect. Feathers smell horrible when you burn them, like hair."

He picked up a feather from the cabinets and lit another match.

"You don't need to show me," she said. "Do you remember how Jack sometimes used to have battles with imaginary bad guys on the deck?"

"Yeah." He held the match at the edge of the feather and the tip of the barbs appeared to melt without even igniting, but the curved shaft caught like a wick and a tongue of fire danced down the feather.

"There are five hundred people downstairs. Fire alarms will go off."

"Do you remember how we used to build fires on the beach?" Daniel said. She watched the flame climb down the feather from top to tip, curling and bunching together into a black nodule as it did so and smelling, as he said, of hair.

"You loved melting my Barbie dolls into weird shapes," Cathy said.

"You wanted to make them into super-heroes with extra limbs from other dolls, but you'd get really angry if I burnt their hair. It was a fine art, keeping you happy."

"You weren't so easy, either," said Cathy.

"Jack hated it when we got too close to the fire."

"He'd sit behind you and look over your shoulders."

"You guys used to make night sandcastles."

"He was so methodical. His castles were perfectly symmetrical."

"Do you remember making fires on the beach later, when you were older?"

"I'd have sand in my knickers and my mouth for weeks afterwards."

"You loved me."

"I know I did. I used to love you a great deal. I shouldn't have said that I didn't ever love you, just because I don't love you now."

The burning feather went out of its own accord, an inch from the bottom. Daniel dropped the stub of feather and took out two of Cathy's mother's toy ballet dancers, a maroon one with no feet or hands and a blue one with her arms reaching high up into the air and her face turned to the side.

"Please don't burn Mum's ballet dancers," she said. She imagined that the blue ballet dancer winked at her as he held it. He kept the dancers in one hand but removed one of her father's miniature Bombay Sapphire, bottles with the other. For fifteen years it had contained no alcohol, but she thought she could smell her father as Daniel's big hands touched the blue glass bottleneck.

He put both these objects down again. He looked tired. He picked up one of Jack's little plastic cars. Cathy could almost see Jack moving the car in the air. The green four-by-four had been one of his favourites. She could see the car whooshing between Jack's fingers; it was hallucinogenic, the car flying through the sky held aloft by Jack's fingers with clouds behind it and water lapping around them, Jack's feet pounding through the shallow breakwater.

He stood up and she kept his gaze, waiting for him to step towards her, waiting for his foot to lodge in her stomach or her spine. She was holding her breath, waiting for the crack of her bones, the familiar ache of his hand over her mouth. She looked him straight in the eye and he reached into his pocket and took something out.

She recoiled slightly, but he stood still and held an object out for her. It was a sea-eagle claw, an inch of brown bone attached to a finger.

"I bought you a sea-eagle claw," he said. Cathy took a small step forward in order to take it from him.

"It's beautiful," she said, holding it. "Thank you."

"You once told me that a mouse's forelimb, a whale's flipper, a bat's wing and a human arm share almost the same pattern of bones, so my hands are as much ancestors of the raptor as a bat's wing."

"Do you still get arthritis in your hands?" Cathy said.

"It's been painful this summer."

"The heat," she said.

"He hated getting salt in his eyes," Daniel said. They were two feet away from each other now, being watched by an elephant skull and a million moths.

"If I'd known he'd gone in, I never would have left the beach without him. I really believed he'd come home," she ventured, watching Daniel pulse his fists. She looked him directly in the eye, didn't cast her eyes downwards.

"He would have done anything for you."

"He never swam."

"You made him brave."

There was a pause. Daniel's right eye twitched.

"I didn't answer the door when you turned up that

morning," Daniel said. "And I'm sorry. There's nothing in the world I regret more than that moment." His words hung in the air. "I was hung-over," he continued. "I was with some girl. It makes me sick just thinking about it."

"You've never told me that before."

"Jack was brave. I like knowing that, at least, when I'm sad."

"We should have talked about that night. We both kept it bottled up."

He kept opening and closing his fists, but said nothing and didn't move forward. She was holding her breath. The child inside her was waiting. Her forehead was collapsing forwards into four thick lines between her eyes. The shape of the space between them changed, became less compact and heavy. He let some air into the gap between their bodies. Her shoulders dropped. The angles and density of everything shifted.

"Nobody will ever know you like I do."

"That's true," she said.

"I shouldn't have come back," he said.

"I'm glad you did, though."

Cathy bent over and picked up the lead toy soldier from where he'd left it on the floor in the Oxo Cube box. When she stood back up they both focused on the small toy man, standing to attention in the centre of Cathy's palm with his pointy hat covering his eyes and his shoulders pushed back. Cathy continued to hold it out for Daniel to take from her. She wanted him to have it and the soldier seemed to stare up at them from under his hat, arms clasped to his sides, ankles pressed together and toes pointing out. Daniel hesitated, then reached over. He took the soldier without touching the skin of Cathy's hand. She could see a damp sheen to his eyes as he held the toy aloft, his fingers around the base of the man's lead feet. Daniel's big eyebrows dipped, his mouth sloped downwards and he had to turn away from her suddenly.

∗⚬⚬∗

It isn't always clear when you meet the people who will do you the most harm. She'd had dirt under her fingernails and was cradling a dead, frozen crow the first time he saw her up close, ten years old, with broken skin on her lips from the cold, and unwashed hair. She was malnourished and fetid and only a child, but his heart had started to beat too fast. He hadn't known why then, couldn't have known. He thought it was because he felt sorry for her, yet he was perturbed by how long it took for his heart to resume a normal pace once she'd run off into the marsh, smashing through puddles, that first morning. You never know when stories are about to begin, but you do know when they're ending.

He didn't look behind him as he pushed out of the office doors and walked straight past Cathy's American, who he now discovered had been standing at the door listening to the conversation. Daniel didn't stop or acknowledge the eavesdropper. Although the American took a step after Daniel as he passed, he must have thought better of following him, instead turning back to check on Cathy. Daniel was relieved, because his throat was choked up and his eyes were wet. As soon as he'd turned a corner and was alone again he stopped for breath and held his stomach with his hands, as if he'd been punched and needed to recover.

He put the bottle of chemical down on the floor at his feet. Perhaps this was where the future began, not in what was salvaged, but what could be cast off. He no longer wanted her constant presence in his head, or the sense of all the different moments he'd known Cathy co-existing in his imagination. She could not bring Jack back. He fiddled with the soldier in his hand and paused as a new sound arrived in the air. It was the soft, then increasingly forceful, patter of rain on the roof and windows around him. It sounded as if the sky had shattered. As the noise gained pace, he realised he didn't feel angry any more. There were other ways to escape the past. The heat wave had finally broken, taking a sigh of tension with it. The air inside the museum immediately cooled down and, as Daniel stretched his fingers, his swollen knuckles hurt less. He took one step forward and then continued down the corridor towards the stairs without looking back, carrying the toy soldier in his hand. He badly wanted to be outside in the cooling rain, walking fast through the streets and away from Cathy.

A *Swallow*

AN ELEPHANT SKULL and a swallow rested on a cabinet of moths, all specimens of natural history that didn't have a place in the museum downstairs. The bird was particularly beautiful, three inches tall, with an ochre neck tapering down into forked blue wings. It had glossy black eyes Cathy could have sworn just blinked at her.

A few corridors over, a gallery the size of a tennis court contained thousands more stuffed birds, so if this one was magically twitching back to life perhaps the matronly pelicans were also preening, the flamingos stretching their legs, the penguins sneezing and the two hundred hummingbirds rustling their feathers ready to seek revenge for the decades in which they'd been prodded and observed. Cathy smiled at the thought and then caught her breath when the swallow chirped twice, its feathered throat vibrating: it was not a specimen, after all. It looped down from the shelf and sailed past a cabinet of dragonflies to land on a pile of science journals.

Cathy was not easily spooked. She would walk first into fairground haunted houses and swear on people's lives without blinking, yet as the swallow looked for an escape route her hands were shaking. Trapped birds, her mother would say, were a warning.

"He likes you," Tom said from the doorway. She didn't immediately turn towards him, instead reaching over a desk to open the window. A low hum of jazz music and laughter lifted up from the party in the museum's public galleries two floors below.

"He's not in a position to be choosy." Her face was still tilted away from Tom as he stepped into the room. The bird remained poised and stared directly at Cathy from its shelf. Tom adjusted his glasses and did the same. She looked new but familiar in her green silk evening dress, as if she'd discarded a layer of herself and climbed out raw. Her hands were shaking and when she eventually shifted her face in Tom's direction she revealed a bruise forming on her eye and a little blood on her mouth.

The swallow darted off across the room again, making them both flinch, still not heading for the window. Swallows were supposed to have excellent spatial sense, but perhaps this one was a baby. It re-arranged its feathers and skimmed off its perch in front of Cathy's face, soaring down from the table to a cabinet full of Monarch butterflies, where it shat a pool of white that dribbled down the glass.

The creature flapped its wings while treading air, its body curled into the shape of a comma. Cathy's skin had a feverish sheen to it. She licked a droplet of blood off her top lip with her tongue.

"Are you going to tell me what happened to you tonight?" said Tom. "I've missed you."

"Is it a swallow?" Cathy said, instead of answering him. Tom took another step forward. "He looks so scared."

"He's just disorientated."

"He's beautiful."

The window was wide open but no breeze entered the room. All Cathy's objects were strewn over the floor, poured out of their cabinet as if they'd tried to escape.

"I was standing at the door," he said. "I heard that conversation."

Cathy didn't react, but picked up a green and yellow Micro machine truck with black windows and silver wheels from an Oxo Cube box on the floor. It had white painted headlights and red brake lights at the back.

"I'm glad you listened," she said and took a step forward to put the car in his hand.

"It's a Chevy four-by-four," Tom said. He pulled down the hatch at the end and then clicked it back into place again with his finger.

"It was Jack's favourite," she said of the car. Tom rolled the car up her arm from her wrist to her shoulder, where he let it stand for a moment. "He was my best friend."

The little bird flew from one side of the room to the other, still not making it to the window. Its deeply forked tail slashed the air. Outside the open window, fine needles of water were beginning to fall through the air, gently at first. The cool rain immediately softened everything and as the droplets gained force it was as if the evening's tension had been let out through a trap door in the sky. They heard the laughter of people running for cover in the city down below.

"I didn't know where you were," he said.

"I'm sorry. I don't want to lose you."

They were quiet for a while.

"The biggest molecule in the whole of nature resides in your body," Tom whispered in the darkness, listening to the water.

"You make it sound like I'm hogging the best atoms," she said. Her breathing was beginning to become more regular. He could see that he might start to understand her. "You won't ever lose me unless you want to."

"You have seven octillion atoms in your body but if we took all the empty atomic space out of you, you'd fit into a sugar cube."

"That wouldn't be very nice of you." Her voice was quiet.

"I could keep you in my pocket."

"I'd be a black hole, too heavy for your pocket." She took a deep breath of humid museum air, trying to steady herself. "You remind me of Jack, a bit. Just occasionally. He was always coming up with geeky facts about sharks and fossils and stuff. He was always fidgeting and making jokes. I'm sorry I never told you about him."

"You're a puzzle."

"You wouldn't have liked me, if you'd known me back then."

"More fool me. I bet I would have." The bird beat its wings, perched on the shelf again. "You don't give me much credit," Tom said.

"I'm always so scared you'll fall out of love with me."

"Why would you think that? I've never done anything but love you."

"But what if you don't really know me?"

"Then I'd like to know you. I'm not going anywhere."

❧

The simplicity of that statement made Cathy want to cry. As the rain fell harder, the bird ruffled his feathers and the air smelt of wet grass and damp bricks instead of matches. She felt almost weightless. Maybe she really hadn't given Tom much credit over the years but she would share herself more fully from now on. Her head throbbed and the bird swooped down to the floor, a burst of energy in the rain.

She thought back to a morning in the Essex marshes when it had rained through the night and she'd stepped out into the marsh before any one else woke up. She must have been eight or nine, before she met Jack or Daniel. The area had been silent, but when she looked up into the sky, a massive flock of starlings was making patterns there. The spectral birds moved in unison as a single animal, turning corners as if they were a trickle of liquid transforming into gas. The birds had flicked their collective neck, playing, everything connected. She'd loved to watch birds making patterns in the sky.

"You missed your prize," Tom said.

"I know."

"We can put your collection back in order," Tom said.

"If aliens on a planet one hundred million light years away were looking at us right now, all they'd see were dinosaurs," she said.

"They wouldn't see me kiss you?" He kissed her cheek lightly, just under the forming bruise on her cheek. "The more I know you, the more I love you."

"A light year is 5.88 trillion miles so they'd see back in time when we didn't exist." She paused and thought. "The act of remembering what you saw changes the neural substrate of the original memory trace."

"True," he said.

"It scares me that memories aren't necessarily facts."

"More scary than aliens spying on us from the future?"

"Yes."

"Jack drowned," Cathy said. "He was my friend for a summer when I was ten. I should have been looking after him. He went into the sea because he saw I was in trouble, but he couldn't swim well."

"I'm sorry," Tom said.

"I didn't realise until it was too late."

She bent down over her objects and touched a little matchbox with a ship on the front, which opened to reveal a pile of shark teeth and human teeth. At the back of the matchbox a strand of neon ginger hair was tied to strand of curly black hair. Some of the teeth were perfectly shaped and others broken. She held a strand of orange hair between her fingers.

"I used to have bright orange hair. I mean, lurid ginger. It got darker when I was fourteen. Jack's hair was black like Daniel's."

"Are these your teeth?" Tom said.

"Afraid so. Plus some shark teeth."

"No tooth fairy?"

"I didn't want to lure strangers to my bed with bodily offerings."

"Pragmatic."

"Seems sad, out loud."

"We'll make sure our kids aren't scared of the tooth fairy."

"I'd like that," she smiled and wiped the remains of tears from her eyes. Her nose twitched and the bird did a loop of the room again. She knew that it wasn't an specimen come to life, but she still allowed herself to think what would happen in the atrium downstairs if a nineteenth-century alpine eagle threw itself above the party guests in a billow of ancient dust, or the six-foot polar bear stretched its limbs.

"The human brain takes in eleven million bits of information every second but is only aware of forty, you know that?"

"By the time I've finished speaking this sentence the earth will have spun 1450 metres," she said, then tilted her head to the side. "Daniel used to hit me a lot. I was never in a car crash like I told you; my scars are mostly from him, although I was an accident-prone kid, too. I stayed far too long with him. I thought I deserved what he did to me. I didn't know how to get away."

"I love you," he said. "I will always love you. Everything is going to be okay."

"If you drilled a tunnel straight through the Earth and jumped in, it would take you 42 minutes and 12 seconds to get to the other side," Cathy offered Tom as she kissed his arm. "I love you, too."

"That assumes the planet is uniform in density throughout. Polar Bears can run at 25 miles an hour and jump over 6 feet in the air."

"Let's get a polar bear for the flat," she said.

"We'll need a bigger place."

"Butterflies taste with their hind feet," Cathy said and she touched Tom's feet with her toes. Cathy's head felt clearer than it had been in a long time, maybe since she was a child. The swallow ruffled its wings. As she drew a breath of warm rainy air, the bird dipped its neck and launched off its perch.

The swallow rose up and slipped neatly out the wide-open window towards the Berlin rooftops. Cathy stepped forward and watched the creature skim on a line of breeze with its forked blue tail spread out, riding the wet air. She smiled as it pulled the tips of its wings back at the end of each stroke and looped, agile, into the future.

This book has been typeset by
SALT PUBLISHING LIMITED
using Neacademia, a font designed by Sergei Egorov
for the Rosetta Type Foundry in the Czech Republic.
It is manufactured using Creamy 70gsm, a Forest
Stewardship Council™ certified paper from Stora Enso's
Anjala Mill in Finland. It was printed and bound by
Clays Limited in Bungay, Suffolk, Great Britain.

CROMER, NORFOLK
GREAT BRITAIN
MMXVI